DESIRE OF WHIMSY

THE INSPIRATION BEHIND FINDING YOUR OWN HERO

by:
Charletta Barksdale

Desire Of Whimsy

Copyright © 2025 by *Charletta Barksdale*

All rights reserved. No part of this publication may be reproduced, distributed, or transmitted in any form or by any means, including photocopying, recording, or other electronic or mechanical methods, without the prior written permission of the author, except in the case of brief quotations embodied in critical reviews and certain other non-commercial uses permitted by copyright law.

Library of Congress Control Number: 2025907111

ISBN
979-8-218-99477-8 (Paperback)
978-0-578-25268-1 (eBook)

US Copyright Number: **TX0008834979 / 2020-01-08**

To my family, who supported my ideas and inspired me to do my best. No matter how many times I ask them to read an unfinished version, they did it, with a feeling of appreciation. They are the inspiration behind finding my own hero.

Sending acknowledgments also to my supporters for the rebirth of Desire of Whimsy. With humble gratitude, I would like to thank my agent for her quick and savvy response during the delicate preparation, partnership, and all collaborations. You knew my needs and wasted no time in delivering results. I also want to give a huge thank you to everyone that had a hand in the success of reintroducing Desire of Whimsy to the world. Your work was exceptionally well organized and precise. I wouldn't have had such a successful turnaround if it wasn't for you all.

Acknowledgments

I would like to say thank you to my editor Cara Lockwood. You believed in me from our first introduction, and it is because of you that I have made a better version of my manuscript. You pushed me in areas where I was weak and encouraged me to do the work when I was tired. When you said, "Writing is an art, and it takes practice," you were not lying! It takes work, and I commend you for allowing me to introduce my foundation. Cara, you are an amazing motivator, and I am truly blessed to have found you.

Thank you to my self-publishing supporters for allowing me to bring them my manuscript and do the hard part, while I sat back and waited for my idea to become a beautiful design.

Prologue

Holding onto a small, interwoven basket, she gently covered the baby with a light green, homemade blanket that was covered with pretty little pink flowers. Someone had put time into making it. She started kissing her baby softly on her tiny forehead. The baby cried, making it very hard to let go. She knew she didn't want to give the baby up, and she started to think of ways she could keep her—she came up with none.

"Sara, you must leave her here. We don't have much time, sweetheart." Her husband tilted her head up to look at him. "It's an orphanage, and there are more children here. I'm sure this is the safest place given the circumstances, and we both agreed to this. I love her too, but we must do this." He moved closer to Sara and touched her arm. "If we get caught, you know they will take Tranquility from us." "I'm sorry, Impedes," she said. "She's my baby, and I need more time. I can't do this."

"Sara, let the baby go," he said, his eyes pleading.

She hugged the baby close to her and rocked her. She sang a lullaby. She knew this would be the last time the baby heard the song from her.

A noise startled the couple. Impedes took the baby from Sara's arms and put her back in the basket. He put the basket down on the front stoop and rang the bell. Sara wept as he helped her to her feet. They ran toward the side of the building, getting to the trees in the woods as fast as possible. Sara took one last glance as the door to the orphanage opened.

One of the nuns opened the door and looked around, searching for why the bell rang. She heard a tiny cooing sound at her feet. She bent down to grab the basket, took another glance around, and yelled, "Mother, we have another one."

Table of Contents

Book 2

Chapter
1

Serenity

Being an only child, Serenity enjoyed life. She grew up very close to her mother, but she still yearned to be on her own. When that day finally came, she moved into her own apartment and felt thrilled to be living in Edinburgh, the capital city of Scotland. She loved the apartment life of living alone, and everything seemed perfect. Her bedroom window even had a perfect view of the apartment complex swimming pool.

Serenity stared out the window one night, thinking back on the day she first found the apartment and told her mother that she wanted to move. She remembered the time vividly, and it felt like it did on the day she graduated from high school, except this day seemed more like a new start on a new endeavor. Serenity remembered slowly walking over to where her mother was sitting. She leaned down to grab both of her mother's hands, pleading with her to stop crying.

"Don't cry, Mom. I'm not going that far away. It's going to be okay.

I promise I will visit often. My apartment is only two hours away, and after I start this new job, I will be able to help you with some bills and other expenses." She then handed her mother a tissue and started feeling a little sad. It seemed to her as though her mother wasn't as happy as she was about her new beginning.

Serenity's mother blew her nose, grabbing Serenity quickly into a hug.

"I know, honey. It just feels like you grew up so quickly, and although I knew this day would come, I never knew it would feel like such a loss. I don't know how to let go."

Serenity held her mother tighter in response and started crying.

She pulled back from the embrace, wiping the tears off her face. "Mom, you are not going to lose me. I love you, and remember what you always told me."

"It's only you and me in this big world, and when you go out to conquer it, remember home sweet home," they said in unison.

As Serenity came out of her daydream she repeated the same words out loud: "Remember home sweet home." She had no doubt in her mind that she would be visiting home every chance she got.

She walked away from the window and headed to the bathroom to brush her teeth and wash her face before going to bed. Clicking off the light, she ran to her bed and did a belly plop onto it, still excited about the fact that she had her own apartment. She grabbed her favorite book off the nightstand; she read every night to tire her eyes and help her fall asleep. It wasn't long before Serenity was fast asleep, with the steamy dream she so often had playing in her head. The same man was always in the dream. This man she so often dreamed about was also someone she cared about, she knew him and would at times feel embarrassed about having dreams about him.

This night, she saw him approaching her bedside. She felt in her heart that he was going to kiss her. He leaned down and touched her forehead with a tiny kiss and then told her, "Sleep." Serenity smiled. "Are you going to stay longer this time? You always seem so in a rush." She reached up to grab him to embrace a kiss, but he was no longer in reach and began fading away. The loss saddened her, not in a bad way, but more because she felt the bittersweet loss of him leaving a dream too soon. Becoming restless, she drifted into a deeper sleep and was content for the night.

Daybreak slowly crept in, and Serenity briefly heard her alarm go off as she stirred, not wanting to get up. "Always when it's a good dream I wake up," she groaned, yawning and feeling like she hadn't had much sleep. She slowly reached over to shut off the alarm and felt a small breeze across her hand, as if someone walked past the nightstand. Feeling uneasy, she quickly sat up, turned on the lamp, and tried to focus her eyes. She started looking around the room, unsure of what she felt. Uneasiness set in, and she slowly turned her head, looking to the right toward her bedroom door—that's when she saw him: a ghostly shadow was walking toward the bedroom door. Half asleep still, she blinked, wondering if it might be part of a dream, feeling lost between awareness and sleep.

Serenity had often dreamt about a male presence, and while he was familiar, she still felt a little uneasy. She didn't mind the dreams at first, because at times she would wake up hot and steamy, wanting more to happen than what actually did. She welcomed it, and she went to sleep early, hoping for a little rendezvous. Now, seeing a figure at her door sent chills down her spine. Since his back was to her, she wasn't sure who it was or if she was even still asleep.

This moment didn't feel real any more. She wanted things to go back to a safe place, back to when she wasn't scared, but she knew the touch she felt was to real.

"Hello! Is anyone there?"

The man paused but didn't respond. Fearful, she squeezed her eyes shut. Maybe it was just a dream, just a shadow—nothing.

Serenity had not been a good sleeper most of her life; she often had strange, repeating dreams. Sometimes, when she fell asleep, she even found herself floating above her body, in a way that she couldn't explain except that it must be a dream. Maybe now was one of those times, since she felt she was both dreaming and awake. She opened her eyes again, and the dream she thought was a dream was not a dream at all. He was there again, but this time he didn't walk away. She closed her eyes, chanting, praying, "This is just a dream. He's not there." She slowly opened her eyes, and he was gone. She started rubbing her eyes and then jumped to her feet, padding over to the door. No one stood in the door or in the hallway anymore.

"Now, that was a bit weird," she said. Taking a deep breath, she looked toward her bed and noticed that the bed was empty. She wasn't watching herself sleep; she was standing outside of her bedroom door, which confirmed she wasn't dreaming.

Serenity stood there for about five minutes, a little freaked out and wondering what was going on. Why was this night different? She'd never been afraid of the fantasy man before. But then again, he'd never been so real before. The only thing different about that day that she could think of was the fact that it was her twenty-fifth birthday; every year on her birthday, something weird happened. She felt like this birthday, things were different, in ways that she couldn't explain. Serenity tried to ignore the fact that she had special abilities that allowed her to interpret dreams and that sometimes parts of those dreams would come true. For instance, one time she dreamt she was living in an apartment, happy and joyful, and eventually she found the same exact apartment. Or one time, she found herself floating above her body, and she spent the night watching herself, just to see if she would move. Her abilities also allowed her to take herself places; she would think about the place, and then the place would appear. She was very aware that she was controlling her dreams, as well as the characters in them and their environments. Those little small things had her feeling unique and different, and she welcomed it.

Serenity felt she was blessed with an unexplained gift but wasn't comfortable talking to others about it or taking the time to understand what the gift meant. She just knew from all the experience that it was getting stronger by the year; she wondered if what had happened that morning was part of it.

In deep thought, Serenity looked back into her room and realized she probably wouldn't fall back asleep. She decided she was happy the alarm did wake her.

"Might as well get up, get ready."

Inside the bathroom, she checked her face, staring into the mirror. "Okay, you're okay ... just a bit of a scare, but I will be okay," she told herself as she started washing her face. "Maybe I should get a dog. I'm starting to have second thoughts on how cool it was to move out on my own."

Since Serenity had left her mom's home, she'd never had issues with being alone, but this morning's episode rattled her.

"It doesn't make sense, but I'm not going to keep scaring myself. I've come too far convincing Mom how great it would be to finally start enjoying life. She's done her part, and now it's time I take care of us."

The job Serenity's mother had didn't pay well, and Serenity didn't want her working two jobs. Serenity was happy when she landed a good job that paid her well. It was enough that she could send some extra money to her mom.

"Stop worrying," Serenity told herself. "You're alive, and the room is empty. So just get up and get this day started."

After lifting her spirits with a good breakfast, Serenity wasted no time getting dressed for work, forgetting about the whole morning scare. Before she knew it, it was time to head out. She took one last look at her room, turned, and left for work. Heading to the subway, she decided to make a quick stop for a mocha latte to put a pep in her step and help her focus on the day ahead.

Serenity stopped at her favorite coffee shop a couple blocks from her apartment and felt grateful for her neighborhood. She loved the shop, and if she ever moved away from it, she'd miss it. She hung out at the coffee shop so much that she knew the owner on a first-name basis.

"Good morning, Cheryl," Serenity said. Cheryl reminded her of her mother. She had this nurturing motherly look about her, and she could always have open conversations with her. She was a few years older than her mother, with small streaks of gray hair beginning to form on the edges of her hair. She wore the coolest pink-framed glasses that would hang low on her nose, and she would always push them up as she talked.

"Hey, Serenity ... girl, you look like hell! Did you not get any sleep last night?" Serenity didn't notice she had dark rings from lack of sleep creeping around her eyes, and she truly didn't realize that she hadn't been sleeping much lately. She thought by finding ways to sleep it was helping her, and having those dreams so often seemed normal. Serenity flinched and looked at Cheryl. She didn't want to speak about her experience that morning.

"Not really," she said. "I think maybe it's because I knew I would be one year older today. Birthdays really do suck when you have no one to celebrate them with."

"Today's your birthday?"

"Yes! I should feel little more excited about turning twenty-five, but I don't."

Cheryl smiled and said, "Of course, you should! It's the beginning of legally being able to do whatever the fuck—excuse my language, but since your grown, I can say it." Cheryl then lowered her voice and moved herself closer to Serenity. "You can do whatever your heart desires, so live a little, enjoy it, treat yourself to whatever you think a grownup should have—and have fun doing it." Serenity giggled; Cheryl's blunt personality always made her laugh.

Cheryl handed Serenity her coffee.

"Happy birthday, big girl, this one is on me—one tall mocha latte." Serenity looked around, feeling a little embarrassed because a few people behind her started cheering.

"Thank you, Cheryl. I think this day is going to be a good day after all. My first gift of the day, and already I'm ready for it to be over. I really don't think anything else exciting will happen. Take care, and see you tomorrow. I need to get out of here before I miss my ride. Subways don't wait for us; we wait for the subways." Serenity smiled and blew a kiss to Cheryl before running out the door.

"Bye, sweetheart," Cheryl called after her. "And cheer up, you hear ... I'm sure the day will turn out better than you're expecting."

Chapter 2

Trance

Trance stopped in his tracks, looking back at the bedroom door to catch one last glimpse of Serenity lying in bed. He wished that he could tell her who he was and why he had been visiting her dreams, but he knew that it could never happen—it was not allowed. He felt it would also be hard to explain that he was madly in love with someone he had never met, and even more surprising, someone human.

Even more shocking was that he felt real in her world. He could feel himself outside her dream, even though that was not supposed to be possible. He just needed to know why he had even appeared outside of the dream, and he was curious as to who was making it happen. Trance felt surely there was a reason for it, and he'd figure it out. There had never been a time when he had lost control of his location and purpose. He wondered if his feelings for her had somehow altered reality. Was that even possible?

After arriving to the checkpoint, Trance started walking toward his personal living quarters, still deep in thought. He wanted to take extra time to try and put together the reason for this morning's events. Things felt different, and he needed to know what was causing the change. He didn't want to be seen walking to his room, but with his head down and mind in a daze, Trance bumped right into his lead recruiter, Impedes.

"Watch yourself, warrior," Impedes shouted. "Why is it that the mind is not aware of where the body stands? I did not train you to be a loose drifter. Stand straight when approaching me." Impedes had a way of sensing these things with his drifters, sensing when they were off track.

Trance looked up and said, "Excuse me, sir. Had you sent for me?" Impedes looked him up and down.

"I have not summoned you. Why do you act as though you are lost? Why are you here and not somewhere dream shifting?"

Trance stepped back to give himself a second to come up with a reason.

"I've just finished my last dream walk and was heading to rest, so that I can train more today. I am not lost, just startled because I wasn't expecting you." He was trying to keep a straight face while answering Impedes, even though he was lying. Trance had just recently begun acting out this way, and this morning's episode wasn't the only time things were starting to change. He felt a change in himself, and it confused him. He truly felt he didn't belong. He couldn't explain why, but he knew it was true.

Impedes gave Trance a strange look but accepted his response. "Have you had time to think about joining the new program?

The spot is still available for senior command of new recruits. It could help you with advancing your abilities and force you to focus on here and now instead of being lost. I think it will be good for you. I do not like weak drifters, even more those that don't have a clue to what is required to succeed. You have potential. I saw it the day you came, and it would be a waste if you didn't use it."

Trance stayed silent and put his head down, breaking eye contact.

Impedes noticed the hesitation.

"We will speak on this some other time," Impedes said. "I'm in the middle of transport, heading to a higher command meeting." As Impedes walked away, he looked back at Trance, a puzzled look on his face, as if something didn't quite feel right.

Trance wondered if Impedes suspected him, but then Impedes was gone, his shoulders relaxed, and he continued to his sleeping quarters. He finally made it to his room, still a little frustrated but glad that Impedes hadn't figured him out. Trance pounced on his bed, wanting to direct his thoughts elsewhere. Feeling tired and defeated, he started to refocus his thoughts on when he had brief eye contact with Serenity, and with that vision alone, he was able to rest.

Chapter
3

Serenity

alking through the door just in time for shift change at the Eastside Kremlin Hospital, Serenity clocked in. She noticed that the coma ward looked peaceful, as usual. The night nurse was on her way out as she came in.

"Here comes the birthday girl! Morning, Serenity." Serenity walked over to the sink to wash her hands and then spoke to the night shift nurse.

"Hey, Fancy, you seem more thrilled than I do. How'd the night shift go?" Fancy began grabbing all her personal belongings.

"Aw, same ole same ole, nothing new but Mrs. Peppers vital signs taking a plunge for the worst. Someone didn't change her IV before shift change last night, and apparently, a family member noticed the mishap. Let's just say I'm glad I wasn't around when Pepper's daughter requested manager appearance."

"Really?" Serenity asked, shocked. "Oh, gosh, is she okay?" She began preparing a new bed pan for a patient. "I just don't understand, Fancy; some of these patients are not being treated well, but you know we can't complain. I just try to make sure that I care for my patients like they are my family. I couldn't begin to understand the feelings their families experience, seeing and knowing a loved one is here but not truly complete. I wonder where their mind goes when they are in a coma. What do they think? What are they feeling?"

Fancy grabbed her jacket and started to put it on.

"I really don't know, Serenity, but you need to stop worrying so much about something we can't change."

Serenity stopped and gave Fancy a quick hug. They had become good friends since Serenity had moved to the area and started working there.

"You're right," she said, breaking the embrace. "And you know how I am. I care, and it's always hard not to when we spend so much time looking after them—but I get what you're saying."

Fancy smiled and said, "I'm not knocking you for caring too much. I just want you to stop worrying so much, when there's nothing you can do. Plus, you have a full day ahead of you. I'm ready to get out of here. Let's do this briefing, so that I can go."

They both agreed to move on and started discussing the list of items left for Serenity to complete during her shift. After about twenty minutes, they said their goodbyes.

"Have a good day, and try not to overdo it with your thoughts today," Fancy said. "Everyone cannot be saved—oh, and happy birthday!" She walked out the door.

Right after the door shut, Serenity began her shift. Her first duty was to check in on her favorite patient, Mr. Thomas, who had been in a coma for five years. Something about him compelled her to stick by his bedside, talking each day and describing her every move and daily schedule. She desperately hoped he would wake up. Serenity was not related to Mr. Thomas, but after five years of caring for him, she felt something for him. She didn't know if the feelings were a patient–nurse connection or something more.

After seeing that all his monitors looked good, she walked to a sink to prepare a small bucket with fresh water for a warm sponge bath for Thomas. She went back to his bedside and started washing his face, while thinking about the morning's events. It dawned on her that he had the same build of the shadowy figure she had seen that morning. Could she have been dreaming about Mr. Thomas?

Serenity stopped washing and stared; she had an uneasy feeling when she reminded herself of the scare that morning.

"Hmmm, you do kind of remind me of him, but with you laying down, I can't compare your back to the man I saw standing," she said out loud.

After pondering the concept a bit, she went back to washing his face. Not wanting to put the two together, because it was too much to rationalize, she blew off her suspicions.

"Good morning, Mr. T. Hope you don't mind the nickname I've created for you, and no worries, you don't look anything like the old movie star. The real Mr. T is half bald, and let's face it, that mohawk hair style will not fit you." After washing his face, she bustled around and checked his IV, making sure everything was in order.

"I just thought it would be easier than me calling you 'TT' or 'Sir Thomas' or 'Mr. Tom,' because that really sounds lame, and I wouldn't dare call you by your first name since we haven't really officially met." She giggled. "Oh goodness, here I go, babbling on about your name, and you never seem to stop me." She went to the nearby bathroom to empty out the water, preparing a fresh bucket to do a full sponge bath.

"How about we go ahead and get started with your daily sponge bath?" Serenity blushed as she thought to herself how goofy she sounded, getting all wrapped up with talking to her patient, acting as though they have been friends for years.

Even though his body laid on the bed like a vegetable, to her he was beautiful. He had a look about him that you could tell he had to be some kind of ladies' man before the accident. She couldn't see his eyes but opened them once to know that they were chestnut brown. He had curly hair that would always flap back into place when rubbed, and even when she brushed it daily, it still found its curls. In addition, his package came well equipped—not that she was trying to check it out, but she had no choice since it was her duty to bathe him. Nothing about Thomas seemed flawed, except that he was in a coma, which was why she so easily built a secret crush on him.

The other nurses couldn't seem to enjoy the times when they had to bathe their patients and take their vitals, but Serenity felt different about Thomas. Since the first day she had been taking care of Thomas, she felt a secret affection for him. It was not a weird one, like a weird stalker nurse, but she truly just cared for him and really wanted to make sure he was well taken care of. Maybe it was because she'd found out he had owned the apartment complex where she lived. By lucky chance, one day she was at work and bumped into the current owner, wondering why he was at the hospital seeing her patient.

It all made Serenity believe that they were connected somehow. She had this idea that if she kept things normal for him, he would wake up one day and she could introduce herself to him. She hoped that he too would be excited about the fact that she lived in the apartment building he had owned.

Coming out of deep thought, she focused on cleaning her patient.

"So, Mr. Thomas, guess what today is? It's my birthday, and I've decided to spend the day with you. It's not like I know anyone that would throw me a party." If Serenity were to be honest, the loneliness of her life really did bother her; however, she never complained. Since she moved away and out of her mother's home, she had been lonelier than ever, but she realized that growing up didn't come easy.

Serenity started scrubbing his legs and then his feet. She kept on talking to her patient.

"Really, to be truthful, it has already started out kind of nice. The coffee shop lady, Cheryl, gave me a cup of coffee on the house. You remember Cheryl, don't you? I've spoken about her to you, and well it really made my day that someone cared enough to make me smile. So, you see no big plans, even though I made everyone believe I would have the party of my life. I'm really not, and I'm very content with sitting here talking with you. I hope you don't mind?" As Serenity finished the last bit of sponge bath, the intercom sounded, and someone was calling her to the nurse's break room. It was perfect timing. She took one last wipe of his feet and got up to take the bucket to the bathroom to empty it.

Serenity headed to the nurse's quarters to answer the page. It was a small breakroom that wasn't far from the patients' rooms. When she opened the door, the rest of the nursing staff stood around a small table, holding a birthday cake lit with candles.

"Happy birthday!" they all said in unison, blowing party horns and clapping, hoping she was excited. Serenity stepped into the room, with a huge grin, feeling surprised.

"Aww ... you guys shouldn't have." She walked toward the cake. "I really don't know what to say." Even Fancy was there, and Serenity thought she'd gone for the day. "Just blow out the candles, and make a wish already."

Serenity was so surprised that everyone was there and couldn't believe how Fancy tricked her into thinking she went home. She noticed that Robert, the owner of the apartment she rented from, was there, and she wondered how he knew or who told him. It all made her so overjoyed that she couldn't hold the tears back any longer.

She looked around at everyone and realized she truly was not alone. She felt happy tears stream down her cheeks. Serenity wanted to make a birthday wish. She closed her eyes and blew out the candles, hoping that the one happy wish she made would come true—not just for her but also for her favorite patient.

Chapter

4

Trance

After his run-in with Impedes, Trance rested and then spent the rest of his day training. After training with other drifters, he walked back toward his room. Trance wanted time alone and was hoping his roommate wasn't there. He turned to the group he was walking with to say goodbye. He noticed that they were all lingering behind him and one nearly ran into him. Trance held up his hands to catch him from falling.

"Watch it!" Trance said. "Why are you walking so close behind me?"

The man looked up and tried to laugh the embarrassment off, as he moved to the side to give him more space.

While away from dream shifting, the group all spent time enhancing their abilities with training. Some practiced mind maneuvering by placing dreams in necessary settings and willing the sleeper's mind to that place. Others that had the abilities to do more could go as far as engaging themselves in the dream, making it seem as though they were a part of it. Although there were more abilities, most of the drifters hadn't advanced enough to understand them.

Trance blew the matter off, not wanting to let it bother him. "It's cool. I'm going to have to catch you all later, I have a matter I

need to tend to." They all said their goodbyes and continued forward.

Trance hadn't forgot about the morning events and still couldn't get his mind off of Serenity. He made it to the door of his room and was fantasizing, reminiscing about when they made eye contact.

"She is so beautiful. She has the most beautiful eyes," he thought. He was mesmerized by them. Serenity's eyes sparkled. They were hazel and had a hint of olive, making them the most beautiful eyes he had ever seen. He daydreamed more about the moments he spent in her dreams, thinking of everything he could to make the moment feel fresh.

"I can't stop thinking about her. What is wrong with me? I can't help but think about the way she tucks herself deep onto her pillow, sleeping peacefully, without a care in the world. I can spend hours just staring at her," he thought.

He stood there in a daze, reminiscing about the many visits he'd made to her dreams. He made it his main focus and had taken a particular liking in doing it. He felt himself changing, and he wasn't sure if his feelings were normal for a drifter. He just knew he needed to be around her to feel her presence.

Trance closed the door to his room, thinking happily that he made it before his roommate did. Entering his room from the outside, it looked smaller than it was until one was inside. The open square footage had a condo feel to it. There was a living room attached to a kitchen, and a small eating area stood nearby, which he shared with his roommate. The beds sat at the far side of the room, with a screen that was across the way, providing enough privacy that he could find time away from his roommate.

"I'm going to have to spend more time with Serenity, I want to see if the same events will happen again. I need to revisit her dreams," he thought while bending down to take off his boots. He began to think about finding a way to leave the drifters' world. He wanted to find somewhere that he truly belonged. He never felt like he fit in this world.

He was moving his boots away from the door and felt a small drop land on his finger. All of a sudden, a bolt of electricity shot into his fingers, sending a jolt through his left arm and a sparkling sensation all the way to his heart. It felt as though he was being burned alive on the inside, making him stumble backward. He lost his balance and fell to one knee, and then he saw his friend Delusion hurry over to him to help him regain his posture.

When the room went still, Trance stopped his friend in his tracks with his mind, not wanting him to come close. The lights begin to flicker, and Delusion could no longer move toward him. They made eye contact, and his friend looked at him as if to say, "Are you doing this?"

After a moment, the feeling Trance was having calmed, and by the time he realized what he had done to Delusion, it was too late. Delusion, being able to finally move, came forward.

"Whoa, man, are you all right?" he asked. "It looked like you were getting shock treatment while standing. Here, sit down; I'm a little afraid to touch you. Tell me what in the heck is going on, and how in the hell did you stop me from moving?"

"I don't know, Del," he answered. Del was the nickname Trance had given him way back in the day, from the moment they first met.

Trance looked at his friend, trying to decide if he should tell him about Serenity and leaving the drifters. He took his chances.

"I was just to our room. I needed some time alone to think. I had planned to speak with you about something else later, when I saw you, but I wasn't expecting you to be here. I was just standing here, taking off my boots, and I started to feel something pulling me. I couldn't control it, and the touch was throughout my whole body, like I was alive again; it scared the shit out of me. We are dream shifters, living in between the living and souls that pass through—so how could this happen? The scariest part is that I could feel someone else, like a touch or something, and I felt their sadness. It seems as if they were crying. I sensed it and felt the need to be with the person." Trance looked up into his friend's eyes. "I'm serious, man. Has this ever happened to you, I mean?"

Delusion shook his head and then he stood up and began to pace back and forth with his hands in his pockets.

"Okay! Let me think a bit. I thought that once we become drifters, all of that feeling of having life goes away forever. So you mean to tell me you didn't feel hollow, like your soul isn't missing? And are you ready to tell me how the hell you just did that?" Del looked back at the door, pointing. "I can't keep acting like I didn't see it, man."

"Did what?" Trance said, trying to look nonchalant about it. Del walked closer. He raised one eyebrow, looking at Trance like he couldn't believe he was trying to play the "I don't know what you are talking about" card.

"You shut the door with your mind and rattled this whole room. What else can you do?" Del said.

"I know that we can appear and disappear, but that's about as far as it goes. I never knew there could be more."

Del gave him a suspicious look and said, "What else can you do?" Trance looked up and said, "I don't know—maybe other things." "I can't believe this!" Del shouted.

"Shhh ... not so loud. I'm still trying to figure all this out, and I don't need Impedes finding out about this." Trance felt panicked. If Impedes found out, Trance would be punished, or Impedes may stop him from researching his past and trying to find a reason as to why he felt he didn't belong there.

"Promise me, man. Promise me you won't say a word of this to any one? I have to check on some things before I can truly tell you everything. Just give me time okay!"

"All right, my good friend. All right for now. No worries, I promise. So, tell me, what is the real reason you wanted to talk?"

Trance finally began to relax and felt relief. He knew he could count on his friend.

"Like I said, there was another reason I wanted to speak with you, and it's what I encountered today during one of my missions. I still would like to talk about it, but I need some time to refocus.

Del patted Trance's back and agreed.

"Oh, well, I'm going to go now, but hey, let's talk later, please?

Stop thinking you can't trust me; I'm here for you." Trance felt relief as he nodded his head.

"I promise and will talk to you later, yeah?" They gave one another an understanding look, and Del turned toward the door and left.

Chapter

5

Serenity

After blowing out the candles on her birthday cake, Serenity slowly opened her eyes, with the biggest smile. She was very happy her coworkers thought about her on her birthday. Other than her mother, she had never had anyone to celebrate with. She wiped her tears, thanked everyone, and started cutting herself the first piece of cake.

"You better cut the biggest piece of that cake for yourself," Fancy said, with tears in her eyes. She wasn't sad, but she and Serenity had grown close since they had been working together, and she knew Serenity had few friends and family.

Serenity turned around and gave Fancy a big hug and whispered in her ear, "Thank you. I know you did this, and you don't know how much I appreciate what you have done." She went back to cutting the biggest piece of cake. It was almost too big for the tiny cake plates that were provided.

After about twenty minutes of more hugs and thank-yous, Serenity knew she couldn't stay in the break room much longer. She had left in the middle of taking care of her patient and was a perfectionist about leaving things undone.

"Okay, everyone, although I wish I could stay here chatting all day, it was not my wish when I blew out the candle." Everyone laughed at the small joke and understood what it meant. She left the break room quickly, taking some extra cake with her.

Serenity arrived back at Mr. Thomas's room.

"You will never guess what just happened, Mr. T. The nurse staff surprised me with a birthday party, and I brought you back a piece of cake. I know you can't eat it, but I wanted you to know that I thought about you and made a wish for you." Serenity leaned over the bed, closer to Thomas and looked into his face, grabbing his hand. When she realized the reality of him never waking up, she thought about how he may never have moments like this for himself, and her eyes teared up. She spoke softly, raising herself away from him. "I made a wish for you, and I hope it comes true." Right before she moved completely away, the tear that she was holding back escaped and fell on her patient's finger.

Looking down at her hand, she realized that one of his fingers moved slightly before she moved her hand away. She jumped back. "Is this for real? Is he moving?" He hadn't moved in years, and she thought her eyes were playing tricks on her. She scanned the room, frantic, fearing this moment would never come again.

Looking him over, she moved quickly, leaning to get closer to his face. With her eyes wide open with shock, she started rubbing Thomas's hand.

"Hey, you, please tell me I'm not imagining things. If you are in there somewhere, please show me a sign." Just as Serenity let his hand go, closing her eyes in defeat, she saw his arm move a little.

"Oh, my God, you moved!" She quickly began to take his vital signs and pressed the call button for the doctor's assistance.

"Hey, Serenity, what's going on?" the doctor said, walking into the room.

"Hi, Dr. Carrel. My patient is responsive, and I felt it was a good time to get you in here to take a look before it all went away."

"Move aside, dear. Let me take a look." Dr. Carrel put his stethoscope over Thomas's heart to listen to the beats; he tapped each knee to see if the nerves were functioning in other areas. "So, you said he responded to your voice or touch? Please again tell me what just happened for you to think the patient is now responsive?" "He moved, sir. My hand was by his side, and I know I felt something."

"Are you sure? From what I can see, there is nothing. Look, I know you're still a bit excited about your birthday, and maybe that little bit of excitement tired you a little. How about you come into my office, and let's discuss this slowly?" Serenity looked at her patient and then back at the doctor and decided to change her story. She didn't like the way the doctor suggested she repeat herself, like he didn't believe her.

"Sorry, sir. I think it was maybe because of all the excitement of the birthday surprise, like you said, and I only wanted to make sure I was not overlooking something."

"Okay! Serenity, if you see anything else, please don't hesitate to buzz me."

"No problem, Dr. Carrel. Thanks again, and I'm sorry to have wasted your time." Once the doctor left the room, Serenity folded her arms, feeling irritated, thinking that something was not right. Serenity was now even more suspicious about her earlier discovery of a spirit visiting her outside of her dreams.

"Is his spirit trying to reach me?" she whispered to herself. Eventhough she felt a little scared and confused, she wanted it to happen again. She reached down and rubbed her patient's arm, whispering softly in his ear.

"Hey, you, are you trying to tell me something? If it's you coming to my room, can you move a finger?" Serenity waited patiently, hoping for a response— his finger moved again! She jumped back in shock. "I knew it! You moved!" Now with confidence that she was right, Serenity tucked Thomas's arm back under the sheets, and at that moment she decided she was going to take the rest of the day off, determined she wanted to try and reach him. She gathered all of her belongings.

She couldn't make much sense of what had just happened, but she was relieved that she wasn't just seeing things. She now truly believed she had seen Thomas that morning, walking out of her bedroom door. She shook her head in disbelief and walked toward the door.

Serenity left the room and stopped in the nurse's breakroom. Everyone stared at her when she walked in, surprised she was leaving so soon. Serenity ignored everyone, marching past them and over to Fancy.

"Do you mind working a double?" Serenity asked Fancy.

Fancy rubbed the side of Serenity's arm, and jokingly said, "What's wrong—too much excitement for one day already?"

"No, I'm just not feeling well and thought it would be best if I went home." Fancy grabbed her into a hug, feeling a little concerned but not showing it, and smiled, telling her she would take her shift.

"I will do this only because it's your birthday."

"Thank you. You are a lifesaver." Serenity was glad that she found a replacement. Grabbing her bag, she moved in search for some sleeping sedatives from the nurse's cabinet. Once she got what she needed, she left, heading to the nearest train station.

The only thought on Serenity's mind was the chance of finally seeing the one person that held her heart, hoping that he would wake up after so many years. She was eager to start dreaming again, wishing that her dreams would tell her something or maybe lead her to seeing his presence again.

Chapter
6

Serenity and Trance

Serenity made it home faster than usual. She was excited about what she was about to do and the possibilities of what sleeping could bring. She removed her bag from her shoulder, reaching inside for the sedatives she took from the medicine cabinet at work. Opening the top of the small bottle, she looked at the pills, wondering if this was a mistake. She wasn't sure if she would wake up on her own and hadn't taken anything like it before. The thought of not waking up really frightened her.

Determined she needed answers, she stopped second-guessing her actions and reached into her bag for her bottled water. She walked to her bedroom and stood in front of her dresser, staring into the mirror. With one last blink, she took the pill, turned around, walked over to her bed, and laid down.

Drifting off to sleep, Serenity saw nothing but darkness. The darkness didn't feel right, like the normal times when she fell asleep.

It was usually peaceful, but this feeling she had now was darker and scarier, and she didn't know why. It was like having a sense of being stuck, and the fear made her whimper. Taking the pill took all of her control away, and the only thing she wanted was to wake up out of the misery.

All of a sudden, Serenity felt a calm settle over her, and the darkness slowly seeped away, making her body feel more in a dream state. She then felt a presence; someone was grabbing her arms. She was stuck between wanting to get herself free but feeling drawn to the touch that was definitely appealing to her. Pushing the hands away, she raised herself to get off the bed. Her feet landed to the floor and then she bumped something and jumped back onto the bed, pulling her knees up to her chest. She saw the man she knew: Mr. Thomas. How could this be? He was lying in a hospital bed miles away in a coma. Wasn't he?

Trance stepped closer to Serenity, aware of her fear, and used his mind-maneuvering skills to calm her. The room became brighter, and he walked closer and softly touched her arm. This was something he knew was in his control when dream shifting. He noticed her eyes no longer had the look of being frightened. He stared into them and then blinked, giving her a signal that it was all right.

Serenity loosened the grip she had on her knees. "Hi," she said.

"Are you okay?" he said, noticing that she jumped a little. He summoned light to the room so that she could fully see him. "Don't be afraid. My name is Trance, and I didn't mean to frighten you, but I felt your fear."

Blinking, she looked at him, captivated.

"It's you," she said. "How did you get here, and how am I feeling like this? It's my dream, my room—how this is happening? Wait, how did you know I was scared?" She looked past him, focusing her eyes around the room. "How did you turn the lights on? How did this happen? Please tell me, because I'm starting to be freaked out a bit here."

Feeling like she had just asked about a million questions at once, Serenity then paused, looking away shyly.

"I'm so used to not even having two seconds with you in my dreams. So you know me?"

Trance slowly moved his hands away, putting his head down. "Yes! Well, yes and no. I know who you are because I've seen you, but I do not know your name. I see you at times while dream shifting, just like when I saw you last night. You were sleeping, and I thought that maybe you had seen me as I walked out of your room. I wasn't sure though. Right now you're not dreaming, only because I've changed it. I can shift it to be how and where I want it to be. I'm the one that calms humans when they are afraid, shift it when I want them to be aware, awake them when I'm no longer there."

She said, "But this isn't possible. You're ..." She wanted to say, "In a coma," but she couldn't. She shook her head. "What is this? Are you an angel or something? Wait, what do you mean you walked out of my room—that was real?"

Shaking her head, she squeezed her eyes shut, and he knew she was struggling with the truth.

"This can't be real. You shouldn't be here. I know this because you're unconscious ... in a coma. I wanted to see if I could see you again like I did the other night but didn't believe it was real. I was hoping to make it happen again to confirm. I have so many questions."

Trance looked into her eyes and wanted so badly to hold her close to show her that he could be trusted.

"Believe me. It's real. You are not still sleeping, only because it is my job to make sure you sleep peacefully and change it when it is not. Wait—what do you mean I'm unconscious and in a coma?" Trance was surprised. "What are you talking about? How do you know this?" "I know this because I take care of you." Serenity dropped her head and looked at the floor. She fiddled with her fingers, clearly nervous. "You are my patient. I work at a hospital on the coma ward, and I see you every day. I am your nurse. Did you also feel my touch today?" She paused, watching his face. "Until this morning, I never believed that seeing you, physically talking to you, would ever happen. It's for real; you are in a coma and have been for quite some years. Today when I was crying, I was holding your hands, and my tears dropped to your hand; somehow you moved and touched my finger. It's the reason I came looking for you."

Trance shook his head, thinking this sounded too good to be true. The finger, the shock he felt—could this be related?

"I felt something today, but it was more than a finger touch. It was more like my body was being electrified, and I felt someone's sadness, but I didn't know it was you. I guess I'm more alive than what I was led to believe, but I don't understand it. This is going to sound weird, and I don't want it to frighten you, but I feel I need to tell you: I visit you at night in your dreams because your world feels so much more real to me, and now I can see why."

Serenity moved closer and touched his arm.

"I believe you were having those feelings because your body and mind is in between my world and yours. It is in a state where it may be trying to tell you that you are still alive. What I don't understand myself is how I can see and talk to you. Is your spirit lost and what is causing this? I can't tell what is real and what's not."

"You see me because right now, at this moment, I am allowing you to interact with me. It's a part of what I do. I allow others to see what their self-conscious mind shows me, and I ensure it's peaceful. We have others that make dreams a nightmare, but they are directed when to do so. I just know that when I first saw you, I wanted to keep you safe.

I don't know why, but after hearing I am in a coma, maybe there is a reason for it."

Trance moved closer to Serenity. He felt drawn to her. He held her hands in his. He wanted more but for now was settling with being glad to finally touch her.

"I'm going to figure this out, okay?"

They both felt the need to embrace each other with a hug and came close to doing it. However, right when Trance was about to put his arms around Serenity, he suddenly disappeared. It was so fast. Serenity was left sitting up in her bed, wondering if it all was really a dream. She moved to stand, getting out of bed, and looked down on the floor. She noticed a small white handkerchief with the initial T embroidered on it. She bent down and picked it up, taking a small gasp of air.

"It wasn't a dream," she said, excitedly. "It worked."

Chapter
7

Serenity

Serenity laid back into bed stunded, staring at the handkerchief Trance left behind. It was hard for her to believe what had just happened but knew it was real. She eventually decided to get out of bed and went to take a shower. She wanted to start the morning earlier than usual, she needed time to stop at the library before going to work.

Excited about the possibility that Trance may recover, she felt hope welling in her. She wanted to go to the library to find some books on being comatose.

"I need to understand the meaning of it all, and maybe a book will explain these recent incidents." Although her body felt tired from lack of sleep, she felt a rush of adrenalin kick in when the hot water hit her skin.

She started thinking about Trance and the connection she felt with him, and she smiled. She thought back to the moment she told him he was in a coma. The look he gave her gave hope that she might be able to bring him home. Maybe he was in an unexplained deep sleep; maybe his soul was trapped between this world and the next. She didn't know, but she felt determined to find out.

She wondered if he felt their connection. Even the smallest touch from him ignited a spark that she felt through her whole body. She couldn't explain it, but the feeling was good, and thinking about it made her senses acknowledge that she wanted him to touch her again.

Grabbing the bottle of soap, she pushed some gel onto her shower sponge and started washing her body. She thought more about everything that happened last night, smiling to herself. All kinds of lustful thoughts came to mind when she revisited how close they'd come to hugging—and maybe even kissing. Just the fact that he knew her made the possibility more real, and she wanted him. She became hot and bothered, and considering her sex life was lacking, it didn't take long before frustration set in.

Moving the soap around her breasts, she looked down to her nipples, tracing small circles around the tips, making them pucker at the tip. She started rubbing her hand slowly down her stomach, moving to the folds of her inner thighs, using her fingers to penetrate her vulva. Slowly pushing her index finger in and out of her warm entrance, she started moaning softly as she thought of him. It was getting her over the edge quickly, and it saddened her that it would be over soon; she wanted to keep the feeling going. Giving tiny pinches to her nipples, she pumped her fingers faster. She enjoyed it so much that she couldn't hold back, and it pushed her into the biggest orgasm she'd had in a while.

Coming down from the lustful high, Serenity's body jerked in a sensual kind of way, mesmerized in the feel of the fading ecstasy. She held her sensitive spot, wishing that it wasn't over. She closed her eyes and let the water rinse off the remaining soap. She then grabbed her towel and got out of the shower. Excitement flooded her as she thought about the possibility of Trance coming to life and touching her, bringing her to a blissful climax. That excitement alone gave her enough adrenaline that pushed her into another gear, motivating her to want to get to the library even faster. She needed to figure out a way to communicate with Trance again.

Serenity was dressed faster than Superman could change clothes in a telephone booth. She headed out the door. Before going to the library, she figured she could run inside the coffee shop to get her favorite drink.

Upon arrival, she was relieved to see no line. She looked at Cheryl, hoping that she noticed the impatient look in her eyes. Serenity didn't have time to chat.

"The usual, babycakes?" she asked. "Yes, please!"

Cheryl handed her the drink, with a cheerful smile. "Here you go."

"Bye!" Serenity grabbed her coffee, and turned around to leave. "Hey! You—wait just a minute," Cheryl shouted. "What's the rush? I want to hear how your day went yesterday. Come on; don't you have just one second to spare?"

"I'm sorry. I'm in a little rush this morning. I have a few stops I need to make before I go into work. I just can't stick around and talk today." She flashed what she hoped was an apologetic smile. "Maybe tomorrow?"

Cheryl nodded. "Sure! See you tomorrow."

Chapter 8

Serenity

By six in the morning, Serenity had finally made it to the library in search of books about comas and dreams. She went from bookshelf to bookshelf, trying to find the right book, and came up with very little. She began to become very discouraged and nearly gave up hope.

She put her head down on the desk and stayed there for a few minutes. She closed her eyes and started silently apologizing to Trance.

"I'm so sorry. I don't know what to do next, and I feel that I have failed you and any chance of saving you. I have not had the chance to really tell you how I truly feel, and now it may be too late."

The lights flickered, and Serenity opened her eyes and sat up. She looked up, a little puzzled about the flicker, and then a thought hit her. Maybe she was looking for the wrong book. She always believed in following her intuition. Moving back to the bookshelf, she started searching again. She read every title in the section, starting at the beginning of the alphabet, in hopes that something would stand out. Landing at the letter D, something caught her eye; the book was called Drifting Gliders. Pulling it off the shelf, she turned the pages quickly. She came across a page that had a small description below a picture of a stone brick building. Her eyes grew wider because this building looked like it could be a clue. She glided her fingers across the picture rubbing them over the building, feeling there may be a connection. The building looked as if it was a European-style old fortress; you could tell it had to have been made hundreds of years ago.

The chapters listed stories that didn't sound of her world, yet the book was in the nonfiction section. She frowned, feeling confused that the book had nothing to do with being in a coma, but she was very much intrigued and continued reading. Each story seemed like a fairytale written about dream shifters, many powers they held and how they trained to use them. The place looked to be something of a headquarters used for dream shifters. She wondered what a dream shifter was, and then she remembered Trance had mentioned he was a dream shifter; she continued reading.

"Some say that it was filled with lost souls that had not crossed over, becoming trapped and forced to remain in the control of a leader called Impedes." She turned the page and she found a whole section about this leader. She read his story.

> Impedes, leader of all dream shifters, was a mighty good leader until he gave it all up, becoming isolated from everyone due to the loss of his sick wife. He spent her dying days by her bedside, putting all focus on her, in hopes that she would recover. No one knew what the illness was, but he knew that she suffered dearly from the loss of their child, after leaving the baby at an orphanage. The day his wife died, Impedes's heart turned to stone. He stayed locked in his domain. After months of this routine and becoming isolated, he decided to put all of his time into a new mission.
>
> Dream shifters no longer had a reliable leader, because he was so lost in his grief, so they thought. Although no one would mention it, they noticed that he changed. In time, they found out that he was secretly capturing souls, using them for his own evil doing. He would take those that hadn't crossed over and use them as dream shifters until he drained them. It turned out that Impedes would keep most of the souls at bay long enough and not return them to where they truly belonged. He is still doing these acts to this day. Some souls cross over, and some became trapped, training under his command until the window to cross over is lost. He uses their energy to make himself stronger, as the more souls he keeps, the stronger he gets. Impedes wants to rule the world.

Serenity closed the book; she was in shock. Was it really true, or was this just a figment of some author's imagination? Maybe it was true. Maybe Trance's soul was trapped. Was it too late to return before crossing over? Not being able to accept Trance's phantom state or even if what she believed was possible, she wondered if he was in a coma by force. She wondered if he should have died in his accident. Serenity opened the book again, trying to see if she could find out more about crossing over. She turned to another chapter, reading until she came to a section that said, "Crossing over can go seriously wrong if it's not your time to do so." She read on and found what she believed could help her—and Trance: "Dream shifters are used for controlling dreams, protecting the mind from losing its soul to evil doers. Most drifters in this world are born, raised, and trained to control dreams to protect the mind from drifting to deep."

Serenity kept reading. She came across a page that was torn in half. Flipping it to see what was on the next page, she found a passage on punishment.

> Impedes, leader of the shifters, banned and punished for being disobedient, was cast out to work inside of the recruiting quarters. Even though his services as lead drifter were no longer needed, Impedes accepted his punishment and requested to become the lead recruit master, where he was still required to recruit new drifters and train them.
>
> It seems that none of the other shifters are aware of Impedes's evildoings. They see him as their lead authority and would never cross him. The recruiting quarters are in a middle-aged European structure with white stone brick. Each level is divided among the drifters and decorated to their individual tastes.

Most shifters don't know that Impedes takes full control over their souls. He wrongfully forces some of them into being in his world, all the while looking for that one powerful soul. Once the mind is captured while dreaming or in any sleep state of mind, it can be taken; the body is left in a coma. Most minds return to their bodies, and others are left not knowing any different. It has become one of Impedes's rules to use mind control tricks to keep tabs on the newcomers, so that they might never learn his secret. When the shifters first arrive, they are required to report to him, before being allowed into the whimsy state of controlling the mind of others. They never truly know what is going on.

Serenity shook her head.

"None of this makes sense," she said out loud. She felt the need to find a way to speak to Trance as soon as possible. What if everything was true, and it was happening to him? She started to pack her things quickly, so that she could get to work. She had a purpose now: she needed to check on Trance to make sure his body was okay. She decided to check out the book to take home. If she wanted Trance to believe her, Serenity needed proof. She also grabbed the book she had found on lucid dreams, hoping it had more on dream shifting.

Leaving the library, Serenity started walking down the sidewalk toward the hospital. While she was walking, she got the feeling someone was watching her and glanced back, but she saw no one. Reading that book and the events that recently happened had her a little spooked. Not wanting to waste anymore time, she started to run the little bit of the way left toward work. She finally made it to the building, out of breath but feeling a little at ease.

Chapter
9

Serenity

Serenity got off the elevator and walked into Trance's room. She was happy that she had finally arrived. She looked at him. He looked peaceful and largely unchanged from yesterday.

Her phone rang; looking at the screen, she noticed that it was her mother. She remembered that she needed to ask her some questions. Serenity figured maybe her mother knew something that she wasn't telling her.

"Hey, Mom!"

"Serenity, darling, how are you—oh, and happy late birthday! Did you like your gift?"

"What gift? Mom, I told you that you didn't have to get me a gift this year! Paying the deposit on my apartment meant a lot, Mom, and I plan to still pay you back."

"Sweetheart, you know you are my only daughter, and you mean the world to me. I will not go without showing you how much I'll always love you."

"Thanks, Mom. I haven't received the gift, yet, but hopefully it's sitting in my mailbox. I'll check when I get off today. Mom?" Serenity whispered, looking around to make sure no one was nearby. "I have something I wanted to ask you."

"What is it, dear? You know that you can ask me anything. Is this about your biological parents, again? I told you that they never cared to be in your life, and I don't know where they could be and really don't care to go over this again."

"Calm down, Mom. I wish I knew my background, but that's not what I want to know. I am asking you now, for other reasons. Was there anything strange about me after you adopted me, like strange things happening around me?"

"No! Sweetheart, you were the most beautiful two-year-old child I had ever seen, and I was so happy when I spotted you at the orphanage. Sister Theresa only told me that when you were dropped off, you were left at the door in a basket with only a blanket. No note or address of where you came from, and the blanket is the only thing I have of yours that was with you before I got you."

"Wait, Mom, I'm not trying to cut you off, but do you still have the blanket? And can I have the name of the orphanage?

"Yes! I have it, and you ruined part of the surprise. I sent it to you for your birthday. Just get home and check your mail, okay? I promise it would maybe answer some of the questions you have. As a child, you always asked me where you come from, and I felt that now maybe you are old enough to know more."

"Thanks! Mom, I love you so much and can't wait to open the gift. I will call you later. I have to get back to work, but thank you for calling me back and can't wait for you to visit some time. Love you!"

"Love you too, sweetheart. Bye."

After hanging up, Serenity put her phone in her back pocket and walked over to Trance's bed. She had a serious look on her face, while she was trying to think of ways to trigger movement from him. When she retraced the events from the previous day, she could only remember how happy she was that the staff remembered her birthday. She also remembered holding his hand, crying, and making a wish. Standing over Trance, Serenity's eyes grew wide, and she whispered, "Could it had been the wish, or was it my voice? Hey, you, can you hear me? If you would just do anything, it would give me hope." She pulled a chair close and sat back but saw no movement. Serenity spoke softly to Trance, telling him the events of her day. This was something she did on a daily basis, but today she hoped her voice would be heard. Although she wasn't getting the response she was looking for, after what had happened at the library and after the talk with her mom, she was still hopeful.

Serenity had been so excited and determined to get to work that she forgot all about doing the shift change with Fancy.

"Wait a minute. Where is Fancy?" Looking around, she didn't see her. She figured maybe Fancy had gone to the vending machines for a snack. And then Serenity saw Fancy walking out of the nurse's locker room.

"There you are. I was looking for you for turn over."

"Hi, Serenity. Good morning. You look a little better than you did yesterday. You left pretty quickly. Is everything okay?"

"Oh! Yes, just major PMS cramping." Serenity gave Fancy a shy smile, hoping that it convinced her of the lie she was telling. "I've always had them bad, and yesterday was the worst."

Fancy rubbed her on the shoulder and said, "Glad you're back. Come on. Let's get this turn over done so I can get out of here. I'm beat."

Serenity finished her talk with Fancy and went straight into her daily tasks. She wanted the day to go by quickly, so she could get home to what was waiting for her from her mother.

Before she knew it, her lunch break had arrived. She was tired and happy for a break. After cleaning and putting up supplies, she headed toward the breakroom. Staring at the far corner window, Serenity walked toward the table, wanting some alone time.

"Perfect, no one's here. Just the spot I need," she whispered to herself, after opening her backpack to retrieve her PB&J protein box. She then took out the library book and remembered how she needed to find out more about dream shifting.

Grabbing her sandwich, she took a bite and moaned. She was hungrier than she thought. Opening the book, she started flipping through the first few pages. She stopped at the Contents page and read the names of the chapters. Serenity stopped when she seen the title "Lucid Dreams." It didn't use the term dream shifting, but it piqued her curiosity. She turned to the chapter.

> A lucid dream is a dream during which the dreamer is aware of dreaming. Throughout the lucid dreaming, the dreamer may be able to apply some degree of control over the dream characters and environment. The dreamer can force others into their dream, directing it toward whatever act. The dreamer is aware that they are dreaming and has a clear memory of the waking world. Etymology: Four signs that dreamers are being aware that they are dreaming

1. Awareness of the dream state
2. Memory functions, self with the capacity to make decisions
3. Mindfulness of dream environment
4. Can pull characters through dimensions

Serenity scanned her fingers over the pages, astounded at what she was reading.

"This is way over my head, but it sounds just like me. I can actually do these things. I wonder if I'm pulling Trance into my dreams." She quickly closed the book. "I have to get home to see what my mother sent me. Where did I come from? Who am I?"

Breezing through the rest of the day, Serenity wasted no time packing up to head home when her shift was done. She took one last glance at Trance before exiting. She hadn't seen any movement throughout the day but was hopeful.

She whispered softly, "I haven't given up; don't worry."

Chapter

10

Trance

Instead of training, Trance remained in his room, slumped in a chair in the corner. He couldn't focus. He was very frustrated about the conversation he had with Serenity, concerning his body sitting at a hospital in a coma. He leaned his head back, thinking. How could it be him, in a coma in her world, yet still his body was here in his? He couldn't comprehend the idea that he was human; he had always been told he was a spirit in his world. Unclear of what do next, Trance slumped deeper into his chair. He really wanted to get back to Serenity to find out more.

Trance knew going outside of his duties was taking a risk, but he didn't care. The importance of being a shifter was no longer real for him. He wanted the truth. He stood and started pacing the his room. "Am I really a dream shifter, or has my spirit somehow left my body? How could this be? All this time of believing what they told me, and now this." He was frustrated and angry and no longer had faith in what Impedes had been telling him was the truth. "I need to know more. I need to see her now."

Trance stopped pacing and stood still, his shoulders now straight; he felt a renewed sense of purpose. He knew that he was going to do it. Trance was going to try to get to Serenity.

He closed his eyes, like he normally did before shifting in between dimensions. A light flashed around his body, and then his body left the spot where he stood. He materialized in front of the door to Serenity's room and walked through it.

Trance saw Serenity standing in her bedroom, and he watched as she slowly removed herself from her bed. She didn't show signs that she could see or feel him. Trance continued watching. Even though he didn't want to impose on her, he stared at her, watching her every move. When he realized she was walking into the bathroom to take a shower, he backed off and left the room to wait until she was finished. After thirty minutes, he noticed she was grabbing things in a rush, and then she left her home. He immediately began to follow her.

They ended up at a train station; Trance sat with her on the train.

Serenity sat toward the back, across from a man who stared at her. Trance became very annoyed at the man, angry that he was staring at her. He realized her beauty was even more powerful than when he originally laid eyes on her.

Finally the train came to a stop. Serenity got off and started walking toward the exit of the train station. Trance stayed close to her, watching her walk down the street and go into a coffee shop. Becoming frustrated, he was wondering how long she planned to be at this shop. He was about to give up until he saw her on the move again, leaving the shop with great urgency. After another brief walk, he watched her go into a library; he was curious as to what she was going in there for. Maybe it was his chance to find more information on what was going on with him.

Trance followed Serenity around until she took a seat. He watched her lay her head down on the table, noticing the defeated look in her face. He knew at that moment that he wanted to help her find the book. While she was looking at books, he noticed a book she kept passing over. Trance thought that book would be a good start, and he needed a way to get her to notice it. He went over to the book and used his strength to rattle it, hoping it would fall, but he was only able to flicker the lights. He watched her stand up, turn toward where he was standing, and then reach for the book.

Trance stood back and moved to stand behind Serenity. It was frightening to see stories in the book about Impedes. He wasn't sure if what he was reading was true, but he decided he would keep looking until she was done researching. He felt a slight relief that maybe this book will lead him to answers.

After watching Serenity check the book out, he followed her as she left the library and walked down the street, eventually arriving at a building he didn't recognize. The destination this time made him feel a little different; a closeness of some sort that he couldn't explain came over him, making him feel as though he needed to be there.

He appeared in a room, standing to the side of Serenity, noticing that her facial expression had changed from energetic to sad. Trance realized she was standing at a patient's bedside—his bedside. There he lay, in a coma.

Serenity had been right when she told him that his body was

somewhere else and he truly was from her world. He tried to touch himself, but nothing happened. Trance realized that the powers that he had only worked on others, not on himself; this brought on a sense of loss and confusion. He couldn't quite come to grips with what was unfolding in front of him. Realization hitting him fast and hard, Trance took a step back and removed himself from the room. He evaporated into the darkness.

Trance ended up back at his living quarters, lost and confused, not knowing what to do next, and fearing that Impedes would stop him. The only things on his mind were escape and Serenity. He didn't know if it was a good time to involve Del, but wanted so badly to take his chances. He figured he needed to think things through first, since he didn't know how much time was left with getting back to his human body. What was important now was finding out a way to fix the situation.

Trance walked over to Del's room, checking to see if he was in. He was hoping his friend could help him figure out how to get into the trainer library. He believed that it must have a record of some sort and hoped to find anything that would explain how he got to where he was.

Relaxing his mind, Trance started putting together a plan. First, he wanted to have a talk with the only friend he could trust, hoping that his instincts were correct. He then wanted to keep watch until he figured out the times when Impedes's office would be unattended. Exhaustion kicked in, and Trance decided he would get a fresh start with finding Del later, but he knew that he would think clearer once he had the chance to rest his mind. He decided to lay down and rest. He had had a very long morning, and for some reason, his energy was lower than normal. Trance wasn't sure what was causing the fatigue. As he lay on his bed, thinking, he closed his eyes, trying to relax. He wanted more time with Serenity. He felt the need to at least tell her thank you. He didn't understand it, but his feelings felt stronger when she was around. She gave him a sense of life purpose.

He wanted to have her in his life permanently, but in order for that to happen, he had to find a way back to her world.

Chapter

11

Trance

Del walked into his room and spotted Trance sitting in the kitchen area.

"There you are," Del said while he moved closer to him, sitting down in the chair across from him. "I've been looking all over for you. You were not responding to any of the beckoning calls for shifters duty today, and it had me worried. I had the hardest time distracting Impedes from focusing on your absence."

"Thank you, Del. At this moment, I can use all the help I can get." Del looked at him and said, "What do you mean you need help?" Trance got up out of his seat and started moving toward the door, telling Del to follow him. Trance no longer trusted or believed their room had privacy. He wanted to tell him what he had been doing and explain all of his recent events, hoping he could trust his good friend with the news. Conflicted with wanting to involve Del, he wondered how he would take the news but felt strongly that Del would understand, or at least he hoped that he would. Not having any other choice, because Trance needed Del's and Serenity's help, he made the decision that he was going to tell him.

They ended up in an area inside the trainer's library, a quiet room that sat in the west wing of the building. Trance started from the beginning, telling his only friend the events that led up to him following Serenity and how he ended up scouting the trainer's library and any area he thought Impedes would be hiding something. He explained how he met Serenity and the whole episode of finding his body.

"Like I said, I was following her to see if she was telling me the truth about being in a coma, and she was, Del. My body was there, and I couldn't come even close to touching it or even understanding what happened to me. I spent much time watching her. I didn't know what to expect, but I wasn't expecting it to be true. I didn't know how to respond to it; I freaked out and left. Can you believe it, my body is laying in a coma? I even tried to touch it, but my hands went through the body. What am I supposed to do? I have no clue what it would take to get back to myself."

Del looked shocked and said, "Wait, slow down, man. What do you mean you found your body?" The skepticism on his face was hard to miss.

Trance looked at him, feeling defeated, and said, "I knew you wouldn't believe me."

"I believe you. It's just a lot to take in, and I don't understand any of it. But is this related to the thing that happened in our room the other day? And it could also be why your senses are stronger and you were able to move things."

"Yes, I could move things, but none of that worked when I was around my body. I was powerless. I don't know how I'm even here with you now. How has this happened? I can't remember anything about how I got into a coma or any other life except being here. But I am so glad you believe me. I wasn't sure, you know, about bringing this to you. I was worried about how to tell you."

Del patted Trance on his shoulder.

"I don't know where to start, but I am here for you. I will help you if you need me. What's our next step?"

"Thank you," Trance said, feeling relief. "You don't know how much it means to me that you believe me." Trance embraced Del and patted him on the back to show him that he appreciated his friendship. "First, I need to find out what has happened to me. I need to find a way to get into Impedes's office."

Del paced back and forth until an idea hit him.

"I've got it! I've noticed that every day for an hour, Impedes is away from his office. Maybe that could be the time we take a peek. I've been to his office enough to notice a cabinet that sits behind his desk, and it has a lock on it; sometimes he leaves it open. If we can get into that cabinet, maybe it will lead us to all the answers we are looking for and a way to get you back to your body. Trance, man, I'm happy for you but also scared. I don't know what will happen if we don't pull this off. Impedes watches everything we do."

Trance looked at his friend, feeling concerned.

"What if I am supposed to be somewhere else? What if my soul is not rested? I have been here so long that I do not know the difference. What if Impedes did this to me? How am I supposed to fight against him when he has superior rank at this place?"

Del straightened his shoulders and said, "Stop thinking defeat already. We don't know anything yet. We have always been special, able to do many things others could not. It's the way of dream shifting, and somehow you have those powers. You should use them. Your spirit is strong in this dimension, and until you are human again, you should consider yourself one of us."

"Okay, Del, man, but my fear is that Impedes may be something more than what he's let on, and I have no clue about how to stop him. But, you're right. I won't give up. Getting into his office to see what we can find may help, but first I need to get back to Serenity to tell her our plan. We may be able to get the help we need from her side, too. Until then, please do nothing. We will put our plans into motion soon."

They shook hands, agreeing to do more at a later time, and headed to the door to leave the trainer's library. Del tapped Trance on the shoulder to stop him from leaving.

"Hold on, man. We need to be more cautious of being seen together. We have to keep things like they were, so I'll leave first."

Trance agreed and said, "You're right. I will let you leave first."

Before he finished his sentence, Del was already gone. Trance was impressed with his speed and how easy it was for him to shift.

"I have to learn how to cross dimensions without that light," he said to himself. "I didn't even hear him leave or see his light. I wonder if it's different for me because of my situation." Without much more thought, he decided to walk out the door and take the distance back to his room. He didn't want to risk losing energy, since he'd need it to contact Serenity again.

As he was walking, he remembered how he became so weak the last time he had seen her, and he wasn't sure he wanted to try using his powers again so soon. He felt lost.

"Maybe it's my spirit that's allowing me to do the things I'm doing. What if I can't get back to her?" Trance started freaking out and decided to go ahead and use his powers to depart. Needing to get to her as soon as possible, he didn't wait until he made it back to his room. Instead, he drew up some energy to see if he could dream shift, and his powers were back; he was no longer weak. The light appeared around him, and then he was gone in a matter of seconds.

Trance had no idea that he was being watch by Impedes. Impedes was peeking out of the window from inside the trainer's library, as he had just shifted to the location. He wondered what Del and Trance were doing there and what made them leave so quickly. He looked around to see if anything was misplaced. He was impressed with the glow of light Trance absorbed when he left.

"He seems to be getting stronger," Impedes said aloud. "Maybe it's time." Impedes stepped away from the window and left to head to his office.

Chapter
12

Serenity

S erenity made it home in enough time to take the slip she received in her mailbox to the post office, in order to retrieve the package sent from her mother. She finally made it home after a long hour and a half wait. She was anxious to open the package. She walked into her bedroom and set the box down, close to the bedroom door, as she decided she wanted a cup of hot chocolate. She left and headed toward the kitchen.

"Going through that box is going to take some courage juice," she said to herself. She pulled out a cup and filled it with water and popped the cup into the microwave. After about two minutes, she removed the cup; retrieving a hot chocolate package from the cupboard, she added it to the hot water along with a handful of marshmallows. She took her first sip and went to her room.

Serenity picked up the box and went to the bed, setting her hot chocolate down on the nightstand. She stared at the box for a moment, not sure if she was excited or a little nervous of what she would find. She started ripping off the nicely secured package tape from around the box, slowly opening the lid. She looked in and saw an envelope sitting on top of everything that was inside. She opened it and saw a personal birthday card from her mother; her eyes widened as she picked it up.

"I love you, Mom," she said as she thought about how thoughtful her mother was. She started reading the card, wanting to take in every single word of it. She felt like a kid on Christmas morning, opening up her favorite toy, and it brought tears to her eyes.

Dear Serenity,

Happy Birthday, darling, and I hope this day makes you as happy as the years have been for me since you came into my life. In the box, you will find some personal items I have been keeping for you, because I knew the day would come when you would want to know who you truly are and where you came from. First, I would like to say you are my daughter! You always will be, and I love you more than words can explain. In the box you will find the baby blanket that you were wrapped in when left at the orphanage. Stitched inside the blanket you'll find clues about you. Also, I have sent your favorite peanut butter and chocolate cookies, and the extra small gift box wrapped in yellow wrapping paper is the biggest surprise of all. You will just have to open it to see what is in it. Happy Birthday, my sweet, and I hope you find all that you are looking for.

Serenity closed the card, blinking and rubbing away the small tears that escaped her eyes. She went to the small box first. It was wrapped with yellow wrapping paper, because her mother knew it was her favorite color. It was the gift her mother had teased her on the phone with.

Inside, Serenity found a white gold James Avery bracelet with a swan charm dangling from it. Surprised, she started putting it on, happy that her mother remembered how much she loved that place. The next gift was a small plastic container that she knew had to have been her favorite cookies. Her mother knew it was something she asked for every year. Looking down into the box to retrieve the last gift, she became nervous again. She felt nervous, wondering if the clues she sent would really give her answers or not. She stared at the package for a bit.

"Now I'm not sure I really want to know the answer," she told herself. Grabbing one of the cookies out of the container, she took a bite, working up the courage to open the last package. Serenity grunted and closed her eyes. "Oh! So good," she murmured, remembering how much she missed her mother and her baking. She finished up the cookie and finally made the decision to open the last gift, wanting to stick with her belief that this could be the answer to what she was searching for.

Serenity opened the box and slowly pulled out a green, crocheted receiving blanket lined with small pink flowers; it had a tag sewn on that was labeled with the information her mother said would be there. In red embroidery, it said: "Date of Birth: June 21, 1996. Place of Birth: Drifting Gliders Orphanage. Gender and Name: Female, Tranquility Irene Smith.

She blinked. This couldn't be right—"Drifting Gliders," like the ones talked about in the library book she'd read? She threw the blanket down and went to retrieve the book to confirm. Drifting Gliders was the title, but she didn't see any mention of an orphanage. "How could I have come from a place that seems like a fairy tale?

Could it be true that his soul could be trapped in the place where I was born? But it doesn't make sense why the building is considered an orphanage if it's really some kind of drifters headquarters and it doesn't have the name orphanage on the book."

None of it made sense. But maybe Trance could help. Maybe he could make sense of it all. Was she a drifter? It could explain some of the things that had happened to her lately. Thinking about it, she realized she never told him how she could be outside of her body, watching herself.

"I wonder if maybe it all means something. It feels ordinary, but what if it's something more. I have to know."

Motivated that she may have found a connection to her past, she started packing the book and blanket into her backpack; she wanted to get to Trance.

"I hope this is the clue to bringing him back from his coma." With this new information, she grabbed her things and bolted out the door, wanting to get to the hospital.

Chapter
13

Serenity and Trance

The next day Serenity made it to work earlier than usual so that her shift ended early. She felt more exhausted from the shift exchange, but she was excited thinking about all the possibilities of bringing Trance back. She wanted to speed up every minute, trying to figure out her next move, but she still had no plan. At the end of her shift, Serenity decided to head home and relax, hoping a little rest would change her mood. An hour later, when she walked through the door of her apartment, she felt defeated. Walking to her room to lay down, she could barely keep her eyes open. Once she reached the bed, she dropped to her mattress, rubbing her silk pillow covers and thinking how it was the best feeling she'd had all day. Closing her eyes, Serenity began to drift off to sleep.

After a bit, she opened her eyes and said aloud, "I feel you. Why does it feel that you are here with me, Trance, but I can't see you?" The room went dim, and Trance walked forward.

"I'm here, Serenity. I had to see you and wanted to be near you.

I hope I didn't frighten you. I have so many questions and so much to say to you that I don't know how to start."

Serenity looked over to Trance and said, "You can start by telling me how you are making this happen while I'm not asleep this time?" Trance moved closer, touching her face but not really touching her; she didn't understand how he did it.

"I can come to you when you are awake, but we prefer to do it while others sleep, so that we do not startle them. I wanted you to know I was here this time. I can't physically touch you, but I can let you feel what I feel and see what I want you to see, taking you to where I want you to go."

"How did you learn to do something like that if it's not really you but your soul? I would think it would be too weak since your body is at the hospital. I guess I'm a bit lost because I do not understand any of this, but I am willing to listen." She was close enough to Trance to kiss him. "Maybe we can figure this all out together, and you know what? I wanted you here, too," she said. "I wanted to see you, to be near you, so much that it was almost driving me insane. I want to touch you but don't know how or what to do; it seems as though it will never happen."

Trance willed her eyes shut.

"Be silent and let me take you to my place, my world."

In a matter of seconds, they were transported to a field full of light pink and purple Linaria maroccana, with a small white plush blanket beneath a small tree. With her body suspended in the air without him touching her, Trance began to lay Serenity down until she landed softly on the blanket. Even though she couldn't physically touch him, she felt his presence so strongly it was like his body was on top of her. He began to kiss her softly. She embraced him as if she could put her arms around him. She was lost in the moment, but then she pulled back and broke the kiss.

"That was amazing," she said. "How did you do it? It felt so real." "There are many things we can do but we are not allowed to do it," he replied. "Most of our tasks are observation. This, I wanted you to experience. I couldn't wait any longer. I feel so lost in so many ways, and finding out that my body lies in a coma makes things even worse. I can't explain it, really, but I just feel as I don't have much time left. It's the reason why I was waiting for you. I think I have a plan and will need your help. I think I may how found a way to lead us to all the answers we are looking for and a way to get back to my body. I have a friend that plans to help me get the information and clues to why I've been trapped. The bad part is that we do not have much time to do it, and that is where you come in. I will need you to be near my body in case I need you to do something quickly."

"Oh, wow, when will it start, and who is this friend? Does he think he is in a coma as well? Has he seen his body as you have?" Serenity asked.

"I don't know, but he has been by my side since I've been where we are, and he is the only person that is willing to help," Trance said. "I have no choice but to trust him, because he hasn't shown me reasons not to, and we plan to make this happen soon. Do you think there will be a problem with you spending more time watching over me?"

"I can work overtime, maybe stay overnight if needed, and I don't think I will be questioned. How will I know when it's happening, or what to do when you need me?"

Trance was about to give Serenity an answer, when all of a sudden he began to fade away, landing back in his room. With his back flat on his bed, he wondered how he ended up there. Trance suddenly noticed a silhouette form appearing above him; it appeared to look like Jesus.

"You do not belong here, my son," he said. "I am with you at the beginning and at the end, and it's not your time."

Trance was fuzzy about what he was seeing but mostly confused about why, and then it registered with him that spending time with the living was not allowed. He started to believe that this was happening because of the time with Serenity; now he saw that it was a mistake. "Use this time wisely to find your way," the presence commanded.

"It isn't your time yet."

The silhouette disappeared, and Trance jumped up, running out the door in search of his friend, knowing that what he just seen had to be true.

Chapter

14

Trance and Delusion

Serenity woke up rested, all exhaustion gone, wondering if what had just happened was a dream or not. Either way, she wasn't going to take it lightly; now she knew Trance needed her help. "Wow! It seems so real, and I didn't get the chance to tell him about my birthday gift and where I was born. Could it be true that his soul could be trapped in the place where I was born? But it doesn't make sense why the building is considered an orphanage if it's really some kind of drifter's headquarters," she thought. Unsure of what had happened, but excited, she left her place with urgency, wanting to get back to Trance's body to prepare.

Trance and Del materialized into Impedes's office. Trance looked over at his friend, speaking in a whisper.

"Did you see anyone before we came in? We don't have much time but need to find what we are looking for as quickly as possible."

They both started going through the cabinet, checking every folder name until they found Trance's. Del raised the folder and motioned to Trance that he found it. Trance quickly fixed the cabinet that he was in and moved toward Del. They both stared at the name listed, and sure enough, it listed his name: Trance Thomas. They stood there in shock for just a second and then started going through the folder.

"Wait a minute. What is this?" Trance said, reading a few pages that spoke of him in ways he didn't understand. He thought maybe Serenity knew, and it made him want to get back to her. He flipped to the next page, and in bold letters with underlining it said, "A lost soul that has not crossed over." What frightened them both was what was highlighted underneath it: "Stolen difter, was not born as a drifter but is a lost soul that have not crossed over; trapped, forced to remain in the control of Impedes."

Del was getting angry.

"Can you believe this man? He is aware and knows that you are in his chambers wrongfully. If he is such a protector, why hasn't he sent you back? Why are you trapped? I wonder how many others are here. How can we get you back? There must be a way."

Flipping the pages, Del stumbled on more highlight information, and then there it was, everything they had been looking for. They had found the steps on how to return a soul trapped without crossing over: "Drifters must be in the presence of the trapped soul when they lead their soul back to where the body lies. They must be aware and willing to go back. They need to remove their memory, repeat the words, "It isn't your time yet," and will their souls forward.

Del and Trance looked up at one another.

"I wonder if I can do this for you," Del said, sounding more excited. "Didn't you say you knew where your body was lying in a coma?"

Just when Trance was about to answer Del, they heard movement outside the door. They started putting the folders back as quickly as possible, closing the cabinet doors softly so that they could get out and head to their room. When they got outside, there stood Impedes with a not-so-happy look on his face. He snapped his fingers, and all of a sudden, Trance and Impedes disappeared, leaving Del standing shocked and frightened, unsure of his next move. He needed to escape and find someone higher up in command.

Del materialized in front of the elder's quarters and caught one of the leaders about to walk inside.

"Sir, could I have a moment?" The elder was startled and looked at Del, curious.

"What are you doing here?" he asked. "You know that you are not allowed inside. Speak, and speak fast!"

Del handed him the folder about Trance and said, "I think you would want to hear what I have to say. It is about Impedes, and I am afraid he is about to do something bad to my best friend. I need help. If you read what's inside, it will tell you everything. Please trust that I am telling the truth."

The leader opened the folder and read the contents. He looked bewildered and shocked.

"Come inside, fast. We are going to need more than just myself for this." They both walked inside. Del knew time was running out for Trance, and he itched to get to his friend, but he had no choice but to do what the elder asked him to do.

Chapter

15

Trance, Years Earlier

Trance had just left the bank and was rushing to meet his new tenant that had signed the lease for his last open vacancy at his apartment rental property. She said her name was Serenity, and she had just moved into the area. He wanted to welcome her into the neighborhood rather than letting the office assistant or his partner do it. This tenant was a referral from a known competitor, and he wanted to make a good impression so that more businesses would come his way.

Driving a little fast, but just a few miles over the speed limit, he came to a stop at a red light. He was glad that he reached a stopping point so that he could make a quick call to his partner, checking to see if the tenant had arrived.

"Call office," he commanded his car's Bluetooth. As the auto voice repeated what Trance had said, the light turned green and Trance began to accelerate forward. He took his eyes off of the road for a moment, glancing at his dashboard display to see if the call connected. That was when the car running the red light T-boned him, sending Trance into a deep darkness.

Back at the apartment complex, Robert, one of the owners, was sitting at the front desk. He had just hung up the phone from talking to the police department. Just as he rose from his desk to head to the hospital, a young lady walked through the front door of the leasing office. She was walking straight to him, and he knew he didn't have time to help her.

"Hello, my name is Serenity, and I have an appointment with someone by the name of Mr. Trance Thomas. We are supposed to take a look at one of the apartments I electronically signed a lease for."

Robert had a not-so-happy look on his face.

"Yes, I heard you were coming. I am sorry, but unfortunately Mr. Thomas will not be able to assist you, and I have to leave at this moment. Give me a minute, and I will get our assistant to help you. Just have a seat over there."

Serenity smiled and thanked him, shaking his hand in the hopes to see him again one day. She took a seat and grabbed a magazine, watching the man leave, feeling good about her surroundings.

"I think this is going to be a good fit," she said to herself, leaning back into the seat to wait for the assistant.

Chapter
16

Impedes

I mpedes moved quickly to the arrival chambers, needing to get Trance to the chambers quickly to remove his memory and replace it with a new one. He had been working alone in the evenings for the last past three months, bringing in new recruits. He wanted to work alone because he wasn't following the rules, and he knew if the elders found out, he'd be punished.

He had been in desperate need to find just the right soul to succeed him in his plan of trapping souls. He had made it his primary mission, and he believed that soul was Trance. None of the elders were aware, and he had planned to keep it that way. If they knew what he was doing, it would be the end of him.

Impedes carried Trance to the chambers, strapping him onto the gurney that would take his memories. Just when he was about to click the buttons to erase Trance's memories, the doors flew open and banged against the wall with a hard clang.

It was Del, and he was angry; he had two elders with him. They all raced toward Impedes with a mission to take him down. Since the elders were fallen angels and Impedes had not yet received his wings, they were much stronger. Suddenly, Impedes body went flying across the room, hitting the wall so hard that it knocked him to the floor and took him a while to stand. Trance had awakened and hit Impedes.

Del looked over at Trance in amazement and started walking over to where he stood, to see if he was okay. He had known of his friend's strength but didn't understand why he was so strong; he wondered if it had anything to do with him being a lost soul. Maybe being in between crossing over enhanced his powers. The fallen angels now knew that he was a lost soul and knew he needed to get back into his body.

In the confusion, Impedes faded from sight, disappearing. Del become worried that he had escaped but was still in awe of what Trance had done.

"Wow! Man, that was great. I was so scared that we hadn't made it in time." The fallen angels came forward as well, speaking to them, assuring them that Impedes would not get far.

One leader spoke with an ancient accent.

"We will take care of him. We promise you, he'll not escape. We just need to get this soul back where it belongs. Come forward now, please."

Del knew he was about to lose the only friend he had at the time, but he understood that it needed to happen. Trance finally calmed down and looked into his friend's eyes.

"I will never forget you," he said and hugged him.

"Yes, you will. You will not remember any of this when you return," one of the angels said aloud.

Del held his head high and said, "I will visit you in your dreams, if they will allow me."

The angels both nodded their heads. Trance and Del both smiled and said a final goodbye. In seconds, Trance and the two fallen angels were gone.

Chapter 17

Trance

Trance materialized in the room with the angels beside him. He saw Serenity asleep in a chair next to his body. He was so happy to see that she kept her word about working overtime to keep watch over his body. He looked up to the bright light above and noticed the angels silhouetted as they nodded their heads in unison, telling him it was time. They raised a hand over his body's eyes, and he heard them both say, "It isn't your time yet."

Trance began to float above his body, descending slowly until his soul was completely back inside his body. He then saw nothing but darkness and wondered where he was. He began to open his eyes, and then he slowly looked up at the ceiling and around the room.

He turned to his left and saw someone sitting in a chair next to him, holding his hand. He wondered who this woman was, not sure how he ended up there. He slightly remembered how he was late for an appointment and was confused on how and why he wasn't still driving.

Serenity felt his movement and jumped up, noticing that Trance was awake. She immediately pushed the button above his head to call for a doctor. She didn't want to leave the room and risk him going back under.

"Trance! Oh, my God! You are awake!" She began moving quickly to check his breathing and pulse. "It worked! It really worked, and you're back." She went about doing the vital checks. Everything seemed normal.

Trance looked up at her, confused.

"Hello, what worked, who are you, and where am I? Why am I in this room and not in my car?"

Serenity's smile faded.

"You do not remember, do you, or what happened to you?" Trance shook his head. Becoming teary eyed, she answered him. "You have been in a coma for the last five years."

Serenity looked so sad, but Trance didn't know who she was or why she was so sad. It was as if the woman knew him somehow, but he had no memory of her. The doctor entered the room then, and

Serenity slowly turned around with her head down and left the room.

Serenity made it home. Feeling defeated, she opened the door to her apartment and ran to her room. Jumping into the bed, closing her eyes, she began to cry hard tears. She pulled her legs up into a ball position to her chest, feeling a pain in her heart she had never felt before. It hurt so much to feel the loss. She cried all night until she fell asleep.

Dr. Carrel checked once more on his patient. Trance was laying there in a daze, at first not noticing the doctor was speaking. He was in deep thought, puzzled about the first nurse that spoke to him, and he realized he owed her an apology. He hadn't given her the chance to explain and wondered what she meant when she asked if he remembered. Why did she leave so quickly? He had seen sadness in her eyes and wanted to know why. He didn't know her—but should he?

Trance finally turned toward the doctor, feeling a little startled, as he'd almost forgotten he was there.

"Hello, Mr. Thomas, it is so good to see you are finally awake. I am here to ask you a few questions while we wait for your family to arrive." He smiled at Trance. "Do you know what year this is, and can you tell me your full name?"

"My name is Trance Thomas, and I think it is still 2012. I just left the bank, and I'm not sure how I ended up here. My mouth feels dry; could I have some water? How long will I have to stay at the hospital?"

"Well, you were in a terrible car accident five years ago. You had a really bad head injury, putting you into a coma. We have been monitoring you all this time because your friend wouldn't have it any other way. He refused to give up on you, and not to mention the assigned nurse was dead set on taking care of you as long as he allowed it.

"He said something about not giving up on his best friend when you both had a business to run. Sounds to me like you truly have a good friend for life, not to mention the nurse; I think she is part of the reason I believe you came through today, talking and reading to you practically every day seemed to have done something. You're pretty lucky, buddy, and I am going to work hard to ensure you get stronger. Do you have any questions?"

Trance began to sit up a little and then asked to see the nurse.

He asked if she was the one that was by his bedside when he woke. The doctor said yes and they continued to talk, the doctor explained what to expect next. Robert soon walked in with a concerned but disbelieving look on his face, shocked that his friend was truly awake. "Trance! Oh, my God! You are awake! You don't know how good it is to see you sitting up." Robert didn't know what more to say, so he pulled Trance into a hug and asked the doctor how much longer before Trance started rehab. He wanted him back to him old self, and fast. He really needed help with the business.

With a confused look on his face, Trance pulled back and looked at Robert.

"What's wrong, buddy? Don't you remember who I am?" Robert asked.

"Yes, I know who you are. You just look older." Trance smiled, hugging him back. "But, seriously, thank you, Robert."

"For what, buddy?"

"For not giving up on me," Trance said, feeling tears prick his eyes. Robert grabbed him tighter, embracing him with teary eyes.

"I wouldn't have it any other way," he said. "You are my brother more than my friend."

Chapter
18

Serenity

A week passed, and Serenity was just getting around to wanting to get out of bed. After five days, she decided it was finally time to take a shower. She had called in sick, requesting some time off, not really sure when she would feel up to returning. Her boss had no problem telling her to take as much time as she needed.

Every so often, she would get a call from Fancy, but Serenity didn't feel up to talking to anyone and let the calls go straight to voicemail. It was when her mother texted and threatened to come over to check on her that Serenity finally picked up the phone, insisting that she only had a cold and was feeling better. She told her that she had planned to go back to work on Saturday for a few hours and full time on Monday.

Serenity knew she couldn't truly explain the truth to anyone and decided it was time to try to get past it all. She made the choice to get up, shower, and make a trip to the hospital to maybe help Trance's with rehab. Even though she was sad, she still felt bad about leaving on the amazing day he finally awoke. Deep inside, she was hoping that in time he would remember.

After about an hour of sitting at the coffee shop, Serenity made it to work, heading to the employee's breakroom, hoping to run into Fancy. Serenity wanted to apologize while she still had the courage to do it and before she changed her mind, hoping that they would still be friends. Stepping into the elevator, she reached for the third floor button, and then she noticed Robert and Jessica, the apartment office assistant, walking toward the elevator. She held the doors open until they got on.

"There you are! Where have you been?" Robert said to her as he pulled her into a hug, stepping back to let Jessica embrace her next with a hug. "We have been knocking on your door a few times, trying to talk to you since Trance woke up. He has been eager to speak with you, since we told him all about how you took care of him.

"He remembered that he was supposed to meet you on the day he was supposed to show you the apartment. Things are still a bit fuzzy to him, and he doesn't remember the accident, but he hasn't stopped asking for you since he found out that you were also the nurse that took care of him. He wants to know why you haven't come to visit him."

Serenity put her head down. She felt a bit guilty herself and didn't have a real answer for them without telling a lie, so she stuck with what she had told everyone else.

"I was sick and didn't want to bring it into work." She felt like it was only a partial lie and easier to say it to others, since it really felt like she was sick and couldn't function the way she normally did.

As they got onto the elevator, Serenity told them she would be up to see Trance as soon as she checked in for work. Feeling a little betterabout the situation, she still struggled with not getting her hopes up. She looked forward to talking to Trance, and she was glad that he at least knew something about her now. Maybe it wouldn't be so bad to start over by introducing herself.

Serenity walked into Trance's room with a smile. Everyone turned toward the door, and it was like she interrupted something; they all stopped talking. When she looked at Trance, their eyes locked, and he smiled.

"Hello, you must be Serenity."

She walked over extended her hand to him, saying, "Welcome back."

Trance took her hand, with a smile still planted on his face. "Why do I feel I already know you?" he said.

Serenity smiled back, ready to joke a little.

"It is because you listened to my voice for five years while I read all those girly books to you," she said.

Everyone looked at one another and busted out laughing, happy that everything felt normal. They started talking about the apartments and plans for when Trance was able to return home.

Serenity felt happy for the first time since Trance woke up. She realized that a new friendship with him was better than not speaking to him at all. Smiling at everyone in the room, she thought to herself, "Who knows what the future holds?" If Trance's soul wanted her once, she could try getting him to want her again. It would take some work, but she was definitely ready for the challenge.

Epilogue

Serenity woke up, breathing hard because she just had a dream, but she was not sure she should believe it. Someone name Delusion came to her in her dreams, telling her he needed her help, explaining that he was Trance's friend and he had told him all about her.

She remembered Trance had told her he had a friend that would help him, but since he had lost his memory, she never knew what had happed the day his soul returned. She was stuck between wanting to come clean with Trance, to see if she could help his friend out, and trying to handle it on her own. Either way, she knew it wasn't going to be easy.

Del arrived back at the recruit headquarters, hoping he had made it back in time before anyone noticed he had taken a little longer on his task, since he'd taken a detour to visit Serenity in her dreams. It took him a while to even find her, since he hadn't had access to the cabinets with all the information they still held about Trance.

Del had made many trips to Trance's dreams, like he promised, and realized he wasn't getting anywhere with Trance remembering him. He wasn't allowed to bring his memory back, he didn't have the powers like an elder and the elders are the only ones strong enough. Serenity was his only hope of trying to get closer to his friend.

As Del materialized back into his room, he saw his new roommate had arrived.

"Hello, I wasn't sure you would be back before I headed out. My name is Reverie; I'm your new roommate."

Del extended his hand and looked the small guy up and down. He thought to himself that Reverie was definitely nothing like his old roommate.

"Oh, hi, how's it going? I didn't think you would be here yet. I wasn't expecting you until next week."

"I am good. I hear great things about you and was hoping to train with you. I'm kind of nervous about the next drill."

"Sure, I can help you for a little bit, but only if you let me rest up before we start, maybe a little privacy too."

"Sure. The drill is not until tomorrow, and I had already planned to get some fresh air. I've been cooped up in this room long enough. If you would excuse me, I'm going to head on out. Nice meeting you." After the door shut, Del walked to his room and flopped onto his bed, happy to have the room to himself, needing time to clear his mind. He hoped Serenity would help him soon. With the possibility that his soul could return to his body, Del felt positive he was doing the right thing, no matter what it took.

Finding out that Impedes wrongfully took a lot of souls, put Del on a quest to find every soul's lost body that he could. He started by going through all the folders he had stolen from Impedes's old office. He found out he, too, was one of them. He had his own body out there, somewhere, and he needed to find it.

If he could just get Serenity to help him find his body, he knew he had better chances of returning. First he needed to read everything he had found about himself so that he had more information to give her. With a plan in mind, Del finally closed his eyes to rest.

As soon as he drifted into sleep, the nightmare started; it was always about Impedes. Del was strapped inside the chamber used to erase memories, with Impedes leaning over him. He couldn't move, and the restraints were tight. Impedes reached down to start the chamber and started laughing.

"So you really thought you could escape me? Well, you're wrong. I will always have your mind, thoughts, and soul."

Just when impedes pushed the button, Del woke up in a sweat, his heart racing and scared out of his mind. He couldn't understand why he kept having this dream when the elders had said they would get rid of Impedes.

But Del knew the dreams felt too real. Impedes was alive.

Enjoy a sneak peek of **Desire of Whimsy Book 2** of the 5-book series. Can also read many other short stores from authors blog page.

More projects to come and for in reading more short stories, my visit the author blog page at https://spark.adobe.com/page/BJpNBLOP28Uij/ https://www.charlettabarksdale-indieauthor.com/

DESIRE OF WHIMSY

BEING DELUSION

Prologue

Serenity stood near her bedroom window looking out at the soaked wet grass, thinking about how much she loved it when it rained. The rain fell heavier, and the winds whistled. She could hear little raindrops hitting the window, harder and harder, with a promise of more rain to come, exactly how the weatherman predicted. She exhaled a deep breath, feeling exhausted, and thought about the day ahead. Her energies sometimes consumed and soaked her mind with dread, reminding her that she didn't have much more time to relax. Moving towards her bed, she laid down, hoping to find her happy place of quietude once more before it was truly essentially time for her to get out of bed.

"Touchdown," Serenity said with a smirk that showed an indent to the side of her mouth. She fell backwards onto the middle of her bed, landing perfectly where she wanted to and began relaxing.

Something about the sound of raindrops seemed to always put Serenity in a meditative mood, giving her a peaceful feeling. For some reason it also heightens her special abilities. The feeling made her body feel some exciting things while meditating and it made her want to drift in a peaceful manner, taking her mind where she wanted it to be. Breathing as she relaxed, her mind suggested a vision of a field full of glorious purple hues, Heather flowers, that spread throughout that land. Envisioning herself lying in the middle of those flowers, she inhaled the scent. Serenity loved the smell of all types of flowers.

She wanted a perfect spot to meditate, lie still and look up at the sky. She sought the memory of her and Trance's last encounter together. Zooming into her surroundings, she opened her eyes, and she was there, sitting in a field full of beautiful spread of Heathers flowers. She was now in solitude, relaxing all the tension she felt all over her shoulders.

Without notice, Delusion materialized into the field where he saw a woman sitting a few inches away, giving him the sense of knowing he had the right person he was looking for. He started slowly approaching her, moving closer to where Serenity set. He did not want to startle her and decided to use his powers to ease her mind in preparation forhispresence.He touched her on the shoulder, willing her with his mind to turn around to facehim.

Serenity and Delusion's eyes meet for the first time he spoke. "Hello, Serenity, I'm Delusion. I'm here because I need your help and I don't have much time."

Blinking, and having the sense that this has happened to her before, she did not feel scared. Instead, she felt an amazing feeling she could not explain.

"How do you know my name and where did you come from?" Serenity said as she swiftly takes a step back unsure of why the closeness made her feel a little uneased but safe wanting to ask more questions.

"I am a good friend of Trance and I'm here because I need his help and yours, of course. Before he left my world, he told me he would never forget about me, and I am afraid that it has happened. With him being now mortal, I knew it would be extremely hard for him to return to where he was a prisoner without clues in enough time, and I am running out of time. I knew when hissoul descended to his body, he would no longer have his memories, I could not tell him these things because it was not allowed, which was why he was not made aware of any of this. He mentioned to me his encounters with you, and with that knowledge with high hopes, I was taking my chances by coming here to see if you would help me.

"You see, Serenity, Trance was right about his findings and I, too, am starting to think that my soul does not belong exactly how Trance discovered. But I do not know where to start or if there is even a chance that my body is somewhere laying in a coma. It is hope, might and wishful thinking, but after a certain turn of events, I believe I should at least try to find out."

Serenity eyes sparkled. It felt good to hear someone remember what she shared with Trance during his coma state and wondered how much information he shared with his friend. She then started scanning Delusion, giving him a good look over, starting from his head then moving down to his torso. Her eyes drifted all the way down to the big black boots on his feet. Noticing how handsome he was and, she was shocked at how he taller he was than her. She felt insecure and intimidate by this divine being, but not in a scary way. He wore a black leather jacket, black denim trousers that fit his defined muscles. . She realized she had stared at his divine body a little too long. The effect he had on her was a familiar feeling that came withconfusion.

Delusion noticed Serenity checking him out and her reaction made him smile, which showed off his dimples that set just above his perfectly cut beard. He prided himself in his appearance and had always stayed well-groomed, no matter the mission. He knew this reaction was unpreventable to not be mesmerized by his looks, because in his world it was a secret inexorable beauty that each drifter was gifted with.

His smile surprised Serenity and snapped her out of the hypnotized gaze. She felt suddenly shy. She did not understand why she could not stop staring at him and realized she didn't want too but found her bearings to lookaway. She looked down at the ground to gather her thoughts. She realized she wanted to ask him more questions, but by the time she looked up and blinked, Delusion was gone.

Serenity was fighting waking up, as she slowly came out of the meditating delusional dream state, she was in. She began wondering why she could not control her transition as she often did. Her thoughts wanted to keep her in the field of flowers she rested in because she needed to continue talking to the male that visitedher.

"Where did he go, come back please," she softly said as she drifted into blackness, into a now sleep state that was out of her control. Delusion was controlling her mind, trying to remove on small memories that he did not want her to have but leaving enough so that she could assist him. He knew that was he was doing was not permitted, but he was desperate to find his soul.

Serenity woke up out of her dream breathing hard, not sure if she should believe what had just happened, but confident that who and what she just seen was real. She now briefly remembered, Trance had mentioned his friend to her back when his soul was captured, and sensed it had to be the friend that helped him in the spiritual realms. But Serenity was not certain. With Trance's memory loss, no one was able to get him to remember anything prior to his accident, and she never knew what had happed the day his soul returned. She was stuck between wanting to confess these things to Trance to see if she could remember and help his friend out or trying to decide whether she should handle it on her own. Either way she knew it wasn't going to be easy.

***

Delusion arrived at the recruit headquarters; he needed to be back before anyone had noticed he was goon. He took a little longer on his task, a task that resulted in a detour of visiting Serenity in her dreams. It was almost to the point of obsession. He was not allowed to bring Trance's memory back to him and that notion angered him but did not stop his determination to get answers. He was defiantly hoping after finding her that Serenity would be of some use.

It took him a while to even find her; he did not have access to the cabinets that held information about Trance and other souls. The mortal search put him behind, the exploration took long but planned hours. These hours lead to many attempts to Trance's dreams as promised. It disturbed him that he was getting nowhere with getting him to remember him or get the information that he needed. Frustration and fatigue fed his obsession, but he was running out of time finding his own body. He was at the point of desperation and why he started the search for Serenity. Although he was behind schedule, he was still happy with his progress, the thought of all that he has accomplished so far made Delusion smile.

As he materialized into his room, he saw that he already had a new roommate that had arrived. This unwelcome news did not put him into a good mood, but he knew he needed to keep his composures in tack. He did not need anyone suspecting anything of what his plans were. With an irritated exhale of a puff, he walked towards his roommate to shake his hand.

" Hello, I wasn't sure you would be back before I headed out. My name is Reverie, I'm your new roommate."

Delusion extended his hand and looked the small guy up and down and thought to himself he is definitely nothing like his old roomie. "Hello, I didn't think you would be here yet, was not expecting you until next week." Removing his hand and brushing past him, Delusion went to take a seat on the nearby chair.

"I am good, thank you for asking. So, I heard great things about you during my admission and decided early arrival because I was hoping to train with you. I hope it was okay, I am kind of nervous about the next drill bit they assured me that we can lean on our peers."

"Sure, I can help you for a short time today if you let me rest up before we start, maybe a little privacy too. I just finished a shift and need to recharge my energy. Will later this evening work with you?"

"Sure. The drill is not until tomorrow, I was planning to get some fresh air. I have been cooped up in this room long enough waiting to meet you. If you would excuse me, I am going to head on out. Nice to meet you and look forward to on training." Reverie turned with a very enthused smile and headed to the door to take a stroll around the courters.

After the door shut behind Reverie, Delusion was relieved that his roommate was gone. He walked into his room exhausted and flopped onto his bed, happy to have the room to himself and needing this time to clear his mind. "Gosh, I hoped Serenity helps me, she's all I got," Delusion said, as he kicked his boots off, shifting thoughts to the exciting possibility of knowing he may get Serenity's help and his soul could return to his body. Delusion now felt positive he was doing the rightthing.

Things has just never been the same after finding out Impedes wrongfully took a lot of souls. It is also why he felt destined to start on a quest to find every soul's lost host that he could. He just can't do it alone and definably can't while trapped himself. Delusion looked over at his desked where he seen the stacks of folders sitting where he had disposed of them, he jumped to a sitting position in realization of the idea that he had forgotten he had stolen them from Impedes old office.

Very anxious to see what he had discovered, he no longer wanted to rest. He reached over and grabbed the stack and started quickly scanning over the names written on the cover of each listed with a description of each soul known location of its host. Coming to one, he froze, staring at a name that was all too familiar. Delusion's fingers were shaking and he almost was too scared to open it. Label read "Delusion", known host Kansas City, Missouri USA and his mouth dropped open. He just found out he, too, was one of the many lost souls. He had his own body out there, somewhere, and he desperately wanted to find it and now know that getting Serenity to help him was not a mistake, nor was the quest to find every soul's lost host. Now he just needs to muster the nerve to read what is inside his own folder. He wanted to read every souls case listed for each folder he had stolen. He needed to be sure he had more information about himself and others so that he could give it to Serenity. Pleased that he finally a plan, Delusion went back and got into his bed, closed his eyes to rest. He was tired, and his mind and body were simply tired from all the past events. Feeling a serene mind in a peaceful state, he drifted into a deepsleep.

It was not long before that peaceful sleep left him. Soon, he was tossing and turning in his bed. The nightmare began. It was always about Impedes.

Delusion was strapped inside the chamber used to erase memories with Impedes leaning over him. He could not move; the restraints were tight. Impedes reached down to start the chamber and started laughing.

"So, you really thought you could escape me? Well, you are wrong. I will always have your mind, thoughts and soul."

Just when impedes pushed the button, Delusion woke up, sweating, his heart racing, scared out of his mind. He could not why he was visiting his dreams, when the Elders said they were getting rid of him. That dream felt too real, and he now knows that Impedes is still close by.

Impedes was alive.

We Call Her Mother Nature

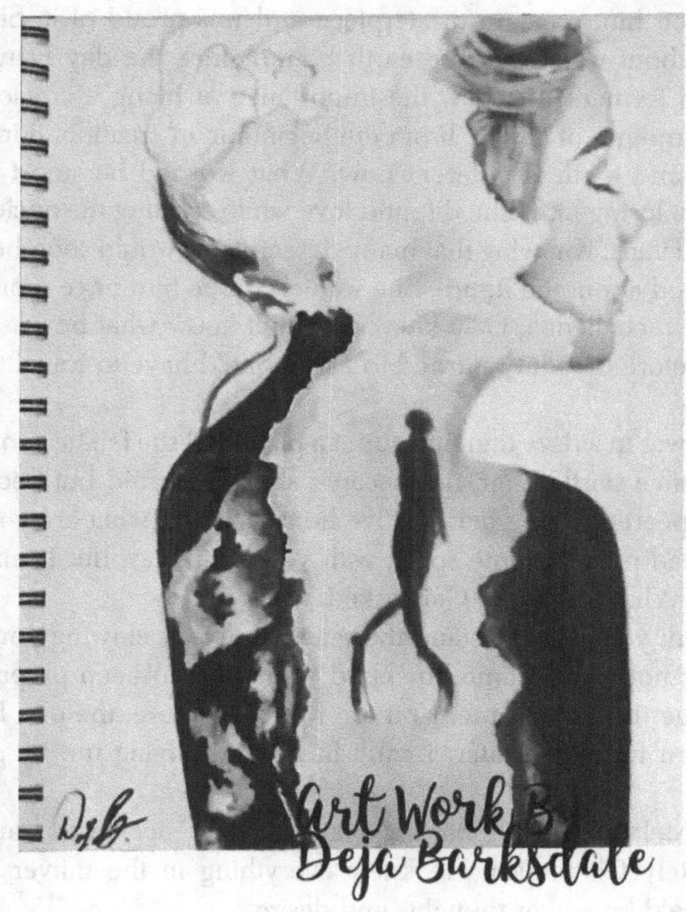

by

CHARLETTA BARKSDALE

The air was crystal clear and from a distance she could see a small little yellow lilium flower pushing through to the surface of the ground. She blew a little air towards it to help it along, smiling as she watched the first stem of the flower bloom. Slowly twirling her finger in a perfect circle, she watched the earth move. It was something she did every day after midnight to keep it in a continued spin. It had the color of blue, a shade that resemble the ocean and a shape of a perfect circle. Gaia smiled, her spirit shined as she thought about her work. She knew she had helped him create a masterpiece and was proud of it. She often thought about wanting to be earth bound since the day heaven and earth was formed but knew the importance of being a creator, earth goddess, mother of all life. From the beginning of creation, things have changed and earth is different now. What worried her most was the thought of losing him. She'd found love while creating the ancient ones they call Titans. Knowing that many descendants would soon be of age, she worried about the future. She wanted to see him once more, but it would be a challenge. Gaia knew he didn't know what he was or who he was before his soul returned to earth. She'd have to travel to earth. Somehow.

Gaia was in a daze thinking about a plan until she felt his movement. His presence startled her, not because she was scared but because he never appeared during her creative hour. "Father, what are you doing here? I had plan to come speak with you a bit later, but I sense your urgency. What's wrong?" Gaia asked.

"I want you to understand the reason I'm not allowing you to visit earth. It's not a good time, my child. You have to keep preparing for the change that is to come. You are Mother Nature, the one I named Gaia, born from rainwater. I can't have you defying me by going to earth."

Gaia felt surprised that her father knew her plans, and then immediately felt foolish. He knew everything in the universe, so of course, he'd know her thoughts and desires.

"Father, how can I defy you if you promised you would allow me to make my own decision? I only wanted to experience the moment before it's all gone." Gaia knew she had upset him, as she heard the sound of rumbles and felt the start of an earth quake.

"I am the Alpha and Omega, the beginning and the ending. Which to come and what I have planned is more important at this time. I will let you make your own decision in due course. There is nothing that is more glorious to experience, than what I have in store. Now, silence, I will hear no more of it."

Gaia stop swirling her finger and put her hands together. She stood 6 feet, 2 inches tall with green emerald eyes and midnight black hair of wool. She then spoke with her head down in a chastise manner, moving forward to approach him. "Father, you know all and you already know that I will defy you. You know my plan before I do and you know his descendant is coming of age. I'm afraid he will not find his way in time."

Before she was able to speak again, he put his arms around her and spoke. "I know this, my child, and I also know that you will return, it's just knowing this is what saddens me. I know what I must do and it doesn't make me happy but it must be done." Before she was able to respond, in a flick of a second her spirit was gone. Thunder erupted loudly in the sky, providing rain for thirty days straight. What Gaia didn't know is that she wouldn't be in human form.

***

Julian was super excited to be on vacation, spending the rest of the summer in in Switzerland with his parents. He thought about it for a minute and felt a little sad as he realized it was the last big trip he would to take with his family before going off to college. He was happy his parents let him pick this place. He'd seen the most beautiful caves and waterfalls and he couldn't wait to take some final pictures to complete his portfolio. When he was accepted into Rhode Island School of Design, he figured creating something new would be a plus if he ever displayed his pictures.

Julian stood up from the rock like stump he sat on while thinking about starting school. He shifted his cap down to shade his eyes from the sun. He notices a rainbow perfectly settled over the waterfall that covered the cave he wanted to take an adventure in. He was dressed in his favorite hiking gear: dark blue jeans and blue pull over hoodie that has his favorite football team logo on the front. He stood over six feet tall with black curly shoulder length hair tucked neatly under his cap.

Julian worked out often. With his well-shaped biceps and fit legs, you could tell he was ready for the long hike ahead. On his shoulder he carried his money-making camera, as he calls it. He made a decision at an early age that he wanted to be a photographer and couldn't wait to start taking shots on this sunny day.

As he peered through his lens, ready to snap a picture of the waterfall, he noticed a perfect rainbow settle over it and decided it would be the title he used for the picture in his portfolio. The beauty took his breath away. He didn't want to miss this shot and started urgently adjusting his lens to focus closer. Lifting his camera to his face, he zoomed in on the shot and something between the waterfall moved.

"Wait a minute," Julian said, moving his camera away. He focused in again and in the same location and something moved. This time, he took off running towards the waterfall so that he could get a closer look, curious about the shadow. He didn't believe what he had just saw something resembling the look of a unicorn. "This can't be true. I thought it was a myth."

When he got to the cave it was to dark to see inside so he turned on the light attached to his camera to lighten the cave so that he could see. When the light flicked on, he saw the shadow step back away from the light further into the cave. He decided to go inside and about halfway past the entry way, that's when he saw the unicorn. It was the most beautiful mythical feathery winged, divine creature he had ever seen. It was white the color of pearl and it had a glowing light that shined around it. He couldn't believe it. How could this be? It started moving forward and it startle Julian and he jumped back, tripping over a rock beneath his foot. He fell backward and his camera flew from his hands, hitting the rocky ground with a thump and turned off.

"No no no, not now," Julian said, shaking his camera hard hoping the light turned back on. Had the fall damaged it? "Come on, don't do this to me now!" With one final shake, the camera came on. The unicorn was still standing a few inches away from him looking straight at him. Julian had visited caves before to take pictures and most of the time he only encountered old carvings, that made great photo snaps he could label and use with his collection. He stared at it and sense a little feeling it was startled or scared. Pushing himself off the ground, he moved slowly towards it to see if he could take a picture before it got away. As he stood up straighter, he moved his camera up to his face and was about to take a picture. Before he could click the button, the unicorn launched toward him, sticking the tip of its horn through the strap of his camera. The unicorn yanked the camera strap pulling the camera out of his hands and down to the ground.

"Release the camera now!" The tiny high pitch sound came from the unicorn. Julian was beginning to think he truly was hallucinating. First a unicorn? Then, it can talk? Maybe he'd just imagined it. He was too focused on the camera, now being held up by the unicorn by its single strap. Julian lunged for it. "Hey! Give me that back," Julian tried to reach for the camera but was pushed away by the unicorn's hoof.

"You can have your camera back, but you cannot take a picture." The beast really was speaking to him.

"Wait, did you just talk?" Julian asked, backing up and trying to find his footing again.

"Yes! I did," the unicorn said, turning to walk away as it tossed the camera to the floor. He heard a sickening crack but hoped against hope the camera was fine.

Julian grabbed his camera, but saw that although the light still worked, there was a crack in the lens and he couldn't get the lens to extend as it did when taking photos. This would cost a lot to repair, more than he had. Yet, he'd have to deal with his frustration later. Right now, he was determined to follow the mythical beast. He headed deeper into the cave. Soon, he found it again.

He was mesmerized by the beautiful white creature, so much that he wanted to touch it but wasn't sure it would have let him. Julian walked slowly towards it to speak again, extending his arm out to reach for it.

"Who are you?"

"I am Gaia." The unicorn's eyes looked sad, and he wondered why. "I am from the Gods. You should not have seen me glow or speak. That was my mistake. I'm.... angry at my father. He did not allow me to be in my human form."

Now, Julian was beyond confused.

"I don't understand."

"I'm here to look after you."

"What do you mean?" He asked, stepping a little closer and for some reason he wasn't scared any more. It was like a calm came over him when she began to speak, a calm that made him feel safe, connected and he didn't know why. Gaia walked away again and this time he touched her, rubbing his hand down the side of the unicorn face speaking once more. "You are so beautiful."

"You shouldn't touch me," the creature warned him, yet, he could feel her hesitation. She liked his touch. That much he knew. "I am not of this world and will be gone soon, so it is not wise that you touch me."

Julian continued to stroke the unicorn and soon found himself wanting to lay his head against it. He felt a connection with the beast, one he couldn't explain. It was as if somehow the two of them shared the same blood. Then, he felt a warmth encircle him, a bright aura of light, and his eyes grew heavy with sleep, and in that sleep, Gaia showed him everything. His past came to life.

When Julian eyes opened, he stood up and grabbed both sides of the unicorn face, pulling it in closer so that he could rub his against it.

"Gaia, is it really you? Why did you do this when you know it's not allowed? You should not interrupt human's thoughts, it could shift things and you know this. It is for them to find their way, understand their covenant and connection with him."

"I know, but you will not remember any of this when I am gone and I had to see you once more. Your destiny is written and your faith will be tested and when I seen the outcome, although I am not suppose to, I needed to see you once more. I was hoping to be in human form but as you can see, our father didn't like my decision and sent me here in unicorn form."

"Oh, Gaia, earth goddess, I will always find my way back to you. I'm glad you came, even if it's just for a few minutes. I am still happy for this moment with you."

Gaia knew her time was up and that it was the final goodbye. The unicorn raised her head up, removing it from Julian's hands and spoke once more. "I will always love you, my dear, from now to eternity, you will always be my first and only love." She then stepped back and the bright light that shined around her lifted Julian up as the aura of bright light surrounded him again. This time, however, the light took his memories. Of Gaia. Of his true nature. Then, the light retreated, and in a flick of a second the unicorn was gone.

Julian stirred awake, sitting up and rubbing the back of his head. He stood, wondering how he made it into the cave with no memory of getting there. He noticed his camera was on the ground with the lenses cracked. He remembered that he wanted to take a picture of the rainbow before he entered the cave, but didn't remember anything else after that. Had he tripped and fallen? Did he knock himself out? Julian rubbed his head once more and felt a small bump behind the lower part of his head and figured it could be why his head was sore. He decided he would not tell his parents, but wanted to continue with taking his photos to complete his portfolio. He'd need to come up with some way to fix his camera.

That's when he looked up at the cave wall and saw a little unicorn with his head between a man's hands engraved into it. It was the most beautiful carving he had ever seen and wished more than anything his camera worked. That shot was worth far more than the rainbow.